DIVE
THROUGH
THE
WAVE

DIVE THROUGH THE WAVE

MARY TOWNE

Library of Congress Cataloging-in-Publication Data
Towne, Mary.
Dive through the wave / by Mary Towne.
p.   cm.
Summary: During her family's visits to the beach on Long
Island, Ruth makes friends with a lifeguard who helps her handle
her worries about the war, an outbreak of polio, and being the
youngest girl in sixth grade.
ISBN 0-8167-3478-X (lib. bdg.)   ISBN 0-8167-3479-8 (pbk.)
1. World War, 1939-1945—United States—Juvenile fiction.
[1. World War, 1939-1945—United States—Fiction.   2. Family
life—Fiction.   3. Friendship—Fiction.]   I. Title.
PZ7.T6495Di   1994.   [Fic]—dc20   93-40999

Copyright © 1994 by Mary Spelman.

Published by BridgeWater Books, an imprint of Troll Associates, Inc.

10   9   8   7   6   5   4   3   2   1

DIVE
THROUGH
THE
WAVE

CHAPTER

~~~~~~~~~~~~~~~~~~~~~~~~~~~~~~~~~~~~

ONE

It was an almost perfect beach day, Ruth thought dreamily, floating in a trough of blue water between two white flurries of foam—the wave that had just slid away beneath her and the wave she could see gathering itself ahead. Only two things would make it better. One would be if Joan were here instead of away at some boring lake up in New Hampshire. The other—here Ruth let her feet down hastily and waded forward to join the rising wave, letting it lift her to the sky—would be if it were still July instead of August.

But no, she wasn't going to think about that today.

"Ruth! Ruthie!"

As the wave set her down again, Ruth turned to see her mother beckoning from the beach. Was it lunchtime already? She hoped not, because they had a rule that you couldn't go in the water again for an hour after you ate.

A whole hour! It always seemed endless to Ruth, no matter how many poems or multiplication tables she recited in her head during the first half hour, when they had to stay lying down. During the second half hour she could sit up and read, if it wasn't too bright or too windy, or dig boring tunnels in the sand with her younger sisters. Ruth didn't really like getting all sandy anymore, the way Betsy and Carol did. Sometimes Carol would let them bury her, all the way up to her dimpled chin.

But no, it wasn't lunchtime yet. Ruth had just let the current carry her too far down the beach. Her parents liked her to stay opposite the place where they'd spread out their steamer rug and towels, so they could keep an eye on her.

Ruth waded into shallow water, keeping her side to the waves the way her father had taught her—one thing you never did was turn your back on the ocean—and splashed back along the shore.

It was funny: even on days when you could barely feel that sideways current, it could still pull you a long way from where you started out. Sometimes Ruth would come up out of the water onto the dazzle of the beach and head toward what she thought was her family, only to find a group of strangers—the wrong color towels, a fancy picnic hamper instead of their frayed old basket, a father with a potbelly instead of her tall, skinny dad.

Of course it didn't help that she was near-sighted. Ruth frowned and kicked at a tangle of seaweed. That was another thing not to think about today.

She saw Betsy up ahead, so she must be almost back to her starting place. Betsy was tossing a tennis ball in the air, spinning around twice with her eyes closed, and trying to catch it before it bounced. As Ruth came up, Betsy missed, grabbed the ball before it could roll into the surf, and said, "Do you want to play Spud?"

Ruth shook her head. "I'm going back in the water. Anyway, you can't play Spud with only two people."

Betsy looked around for their father, but he was helping Carol build a sand castle above the tide line. Their mother had returned to her towel and book.

"I wish we didn't always have to come to Number Nine," Betsy grumbled. "There's nothing to *do* here. Why can't we go to Number Two sometime? We never get to go there anymore."

Jones Beach State Park, on the south shore of Long Island, was divided into numbered sections along its wide white miles of sand. Number Nine was at the far end, with a modest, flat-roofed pavilion and a small parking lot that hardly ever got filled up, even on weekends. That was partly because of gas rationing, of course. But Ruth couldn't remember it being crowded even before the war, the summer before last.

Number Two, by contrast, was one of the big pavilions near the start of the beach road. It had a huge swimming pool, a playground with slides and swings, and a boardwalk where you could buy thin hamburgers in fresh, damp buns oozing catsup and pickle relish.

Ruth's mouth watered at the thought of those hamburgers, but she said, "You know why—it's too crowded." When Betsy opened her mouth to argue, she said, "There were zillions of cars in the parking lot, didn't you see? We would've had a really long walk to the beach."

Betsy said, "Well, we could go on a weekday sometime. That's what the Thomases do, and it's hardly crowded at all." Cindy Thomas was Betsy's best friend, the way Joan Decker was Ruth's. "Cindy says there isn't even any line for the slide."

The tall slide into the swimming pool, she meant. Ruth stared at her. "You mean they go in the *pool*?"

"Well, sure."

But Betsy's blue eyes avoided hers. They both knew that public swimming pools were where you could get polio, especially late in the summer. Polio was infantile paralysis. That sounded like only little kids could get it, but the President had had it—that was why he was always sitting in a wheelchair—and so had a girl at school who wore a metal brace on her leg and got to be excused from gym.

Ruth didn't have much use for Cindy Thomas, and Cindy's little brother Jimmy was a brat. Still, she didn't want them to get sick and maybe end up being crippled. She said, "Doesn't Mrs. Thomas worry?"

Betsy shrugged uneasily. "I guess she thinks if the pool isn't crowded . . . Anyway, the doctors don't know for sure how people get it."

Ruth shivered, in spite of the sunlight and the warm blue air that seemed to pulse and quiver with the motion of the waves. She imagined a germ floating in a giant swimming pool, like a tiny, transparent jellyfish. But of course you couldn't actually see a germ, no matter how hard you looked, unless maybe you had a microscope. Betsy had a pretend microscope at home, made of cardboard. She wanted to be a scientist or a doctor when she grew up. Anyway, Ruth thought, you couldn't take a microscope into a pool.

Maybe Betsy was thinking the same thing, because she said with sudden fierceness, "If I was a doctor, I'd find out. I'd stay up all night, every night, until I found out."

Ruth nodded. Betsy would, too. You wouldn't think it to look at her, with her snub nose and soft, honey-blond curls, but Betsy was amazingly stubborn. Once she'd spent a whole afternoon trying to win at solitaire, dealing the cards over and over and never cheating. By the time the game finally worked out, Ruth and Carol were halfway through supper. Betsy had to have cold macaroni-and-cheese and didn't get any dessert.

Ruth said, "Well, anyway, I'd rather swim in the

ocean than in a pool any day. Something's always *happening* in the ocean."

She stood surveying it with satisfaction, her fists on her hips. The waves were medium-high today, just the way she liked them—long combers rolling in to break near the shore in lacy, dancing flakes of light.

"I'm going back in from farther up the beach this time," she told Betsy, pointing toward the distant lifeguard's chair. "Then I won't have to keep coming out all the time. Tell Mom, okay?"

Before Betsy could say they were supposed to stay even with their parents, not go in swimming off by themselves, Ruth splashed rapidly away.

CHAPTER

~~~~~~~~~~~~~~~~~~~~~~~~~~~~~

TWO

A couple of older boys were trying to ride a big wave all the way in to shore, holding their prone bodies stiff as boards amid the rushing tumble of white water. As Ruth dodged out of their way, something banged into her ankle—a wooden beach pail. She grabbed the handle before the pail could be sucked away into the receding wave and handed it to its owner, a little kid about Carol's age.

Then she angled up the slope of the beach toward the tall, white lifeguard's chair, intending to get a running start back into the water.

"Thanks," said a voice high above her head.

Ruth squinted up into the face of the lifeguard, a bronzed young man in orange trunks with a sailor's hat perched on top of his curly, salt-stiffened blond hair. "What for?" she said, shading her eyes.

"For catching that pail. I've been keeping an eye on that little boy—his folks aren't paying any attention to him." He nodded over his shoulder at some people playing cards around a square of oilcloth. "If I had my way," he added, "kids wouldn't be allowed to take anything in the water with them until they knew how to swim. The pail or the ball or whatever it is gets caught in a wave, and next thing you know they've gone in after it."

Despite his friendly tone, the lifeguard didn't look at Ruth as he spoke. His gaze was on the ocean, sweeping slowly from left to right and back again.

Ruth moved around to the other side of the chair where the sun wasn't in her eyes and said shyly, "I guess that's why they don't allow rafts or inner tubes—little kids could get carried out too far."

"Right, and not just little kids. Stuff like that can be a real headache for a lifeguard, rafts especially. They're fun to ride in the surf, though, if you've ever tried it." He grinned, showing teeth as white as his sailor's hat.

Ruth was about to say she had, just once, at a private club farther out on the island that friends of her parents belonged to, when the lifeguard blew a shrill blast on his whistle and made a series of beckoning motions with his muscular arm.

She turned to see who he was looking at and finally spotted two small bathing-capped heads bobbing in the blue water out beyond the breakers.

"Are they all right?" she asked anxiously,

hitching herself partway up the ladderlike side of the chair in order to see better.

"Oh, sure—a couple of ladies, got talking and lost track of where they were. It's a light surf today, and no rips to worry about in this area. Still, I don't like to see anyone drifting too far out unless they're strong swimmers."

The two women had turned and seemed to be breaststroking slowly toward shore. After a minute, they stopped and began treading water again, but the lifeguard seemed satisfied.

"You must have really good eyesight," Ruth said, impressed.

"Yeah, that's one thing you can't do without on this job—twenty-twenty vision."

"I'm probably going to have to get glasses in the fall," Ruth said glumly, hooking an arm around one of the white-painted rungs. "When school starts."

"Well, hey, they'll probably look good on you." The lifeguard shot her a quick glance. His eyes were hazel green like her own, only with blond lashes and eyebrows bleached almost white by the sun. "Anyhow, you gotta be able to see the blackboard, right?"

Ruth nodded. If they even use the blackboard in sixth grade, she thought, and felt the familiar quake in the pit of her stomach. She'd almost rather think about wearing glasses and how awful they were going to make her look. It just wasn't fair that she had to be the one in her family who needed glasses. Both of her sisters were cute, with rounded, sturdy limbs and naturally curly hair and faces people smiled at. But Ruth was skinny and plain and uninteresting-looking, with straight, mouse-colored hair and a gap between her two front teeth.

Well, of course, her father wore glasses, but that was different—they were like a part of his face.

"I bet you're smart in school," the lifeguard offered, when Ruth didn't say anything more. "I can tell by the way you swim."

"Really?" Ruth felt herself flush, surprised that he'd noticed her.

"Yeah. I've only been working here about a month, but I noticed your family right off because of the way you three girls all wear the same bathing suits."

"That's so our parents can keep track of us better," Ruth muttered. This year's suit wasn't too bad—blue, with yellow zigzag stripes that reminded her of Captain Marvel in the comic books. "Shazam!" she'd said when she first tried hers on, making her sisters giggle. But Ruth hated wearing matching clothes, even when there was a good reason for it.

"Anyway," the lifeguard said, "I could tell right off you were a good, smart swimmer, just like your dad. You don't take a lot of dumb chances the way some kids do, but you're not scared of the ocean, either."

"I'm scared of it sometimes," Ruth felt honor-bound to say. "When it's really rough, or right after I get boiled."

"Boiled" meant catching a wave wrong and being

rolled around inside hard, bumpy knots of foam that didn't even feel like water, with sand getting in your eyes and nasty little shells scraping your knees and elbows.

"Well, sure, and you're right to be. Unless you respect the ocean, it can't be your friend. That's not the kind of scared I mean. Your sister, now, the one with the blond hair—is she older or younger?"

"Younger." Ruth scowled, though it was a familiar question. Betsy was big for her age, Ruth small for hers.

"She never has any fun in the water because she's always tensing up. By the time she decides if she's going to ride a wave or jump it or dive through it—wham! It's already on top of her."

"But Betsy's the good athlete in our family," Ruth said in surprise. "She's really well coordinated. Daddy always says so."

The lifeguard shrugged. "Maybe so. But not when it comes to swimming in the ocean."

Ruth had never really thought about it, but it was true that although Betsy usually beat her into the water when they first arrived—just as their mother was usually the rotten egg—she never stayed in very long unless their father stayed in, too. It was almost as if she still needed him nearby to catch her or tell her where to stand. She said she got cold, but maybe that wasn't the reason.

"My parents call me their water rat," Ruth confided. "I never like to come out of the ocean, even after my lips turn blue."

She leaned out from the chair and gave a sigh of contentment as she surveyed the scene around her—the dimpled expanse of sand dotted with the bright colors of towels and bathing suits and an occasional striped umbrella, the sparkling blue water crisped with white beneath a paler blue sky.

"I wish I could always be at the beach," she told the lifeguard. "It's my favorite place in the whole world."

"And you'd like it always to be summer, too, right?" He chuckled. "Yeah, I know what you mean."

Something in his voice made Ruth swing around to look up at his face. But just then he noticed a bunch of big boys trying to duck each other in the surf—or maybe he'd been watching them all along, Ruth thought humbly, aware that his attention had been only partly focused on her.

He picked up his megaphone and called through it, "Enough horsing around there!" The boys looked around, startled. Sheepishly, they separated, then made a show of racing each other out into deeper water, whooping and bellyflopping through the waves.

Ruth dropped down onto the sand, feeling a little sheepish, too. She'd been ready to tell the lifeguard about her special reason for wishing fall would never come this year—because of skipping a grade in school and having to make a whole lot of new friends, something she was afraid she wouldn't be any good at, especially if she had to wear glasses.

But probably he wouldn't be interested; probably he'd just been talking to her to pass the time. It must get lonely, Ruth thought, sitting up in that tall chair all day, while the people on the beach were free to chat and wander around and toss beach balls back and forth and run races along the hard sand at the water's edge.

She had turned away and was squaring her shoulders for her dash into the ocean when the lifeguard called down, "Say, what's your name? I need to know what to call you next time."

"It's Ruth," she said, feeling a little glow of pleasure. Next time. So he really was being friendly, not just feeling bored, or worse, sorry for her, a funny-looking girl who might be a good swimmer but who was also shrimpy and skinny and not as cute as her sisters.

"Mine's Russell," he told her. "Russ, for short. I guess you don't need a nickname, though—not with a short name like Ruth."

It was funny, the way he had of picking on things that bothered her. Ruth wished she *did* have a nickname, the way Betsy was short for Elizabeth and Carol was sometimes called Carrie or Caro. But there was nothing you could do with a plain name like Ruth.

"People call me Ruthie sometimes," she said reluctantly. "Even my mother, if she forgets. But I hate it."

"Ruthie for long, hey? Okay, I'll remember—just Ruth."

He smiled, but his eyes were scanning the ocean again. Ruth hesitated a moment, then took a deep breath and sprinted for the water, knowing how cold it was going to feel after such a long time out in the sun. Without pausing, she splashed through the foam, dove through a small wave, swam hard, and did a porpoise dive under another, bigger wave, aiming deep for its powerful, gleaming roots.

Then she couldn't help turning her head to see if Russ had been watching. But there was no way to tell. He was sitting back in the chair with his arms folded, his head swiveling slowly from side to side, keeping all the swimmers safe.

CHAPTER

~~~~~~~~~~~~~~~~~~~~

THREE

Ruth knew she was lucky that her family lived only fifteen miles from the ocean, an easy drive along the flat Long Island roads in their old gray Ford. It was lucky, too, that her father could take the train every day to his job in the city, so they could save their gasoline for the beach.

Still, she always dreaded the trip home, with everyone crammed together in the hot car, all sticky and sandy and cross. Today it was Ruth's turn to sit in the middle of the backseat. Carol was a sleepy, heavy lump on one side of her, while Betsy kept crowding her on the other, chanting, "Ruthie has a crush, Ruthie has a crush," even after their parents told her to stop. They'd all noticed her talking to the lifeguard.

"I hope you weren't bothering him, Ruth," her

father said. "That job takes full-time concentration, you know." He had been a lifeguard years ago, at some lake in upstate New York.

"Oh, he was watching the ocean the whole time," Ruth assured him.

"It must get lonely, sitting up on that platform all by himself," her mother remarked. This was what Ruth had thought, but somehow she didn't like her mother saying it.

"Well, it's what he's paid to do," Mr. Owen said grumpily, stamping on the brakes to let a large, sunburned family cross the road in front of them. They were laden with folding chairs and portable radios and other paraphernalia the Owens considered unnecessary for the beach. "He's lucky the draft hasn't caught up with him."

Ruth hadn't thought about that. She frowned, hoping it wouldn't.

Betsy poked her in the ribs. Annoyed, Ruth started to poke her back, then saw what Betsy was looking at: the giant swimming pool at Number Two, clearly visible from the road behind its tall chain-link fence.

Silently, they gazed at all the kids frolicking and splashing and yelling and having fun, when all the time a single drop of water—a drop that looked just like every other drop of water—might land on them, with poison in it.

It was the scariest thought Ruth had ever had, even scarier than thinking about the third rail on the train tracks.

As usual, though, she cheered up once they turned into the leafy streets of their town, where people were outside watering their lawns and throwing balls for their dogs and playing lazy Saturday-afternoon games of badminton in side yards.

After she'd washed away the salt and sand and put on a clean polo shirt and shorts, there was even something magical about going out into her own familiar backyard. The grass felt silky and cool beneath her feet, and the air was deliciously soft against her skin. Tonight they were having an early picnic supper, the way they often did after a day at the beach—potato salad with thin-sliced cold cuts and thicker-sliced tomatoes from the Victory Garden beyond the garage.

Also, it was tonight that Ruth was finally getting to call her friend Joan long-distance in New Hampshire. The Deckers were away for a month, and the two sets of parents had agreed on one telephone call apiece, three minutes at a time.

"Hello, there, Ruthie. My, how brown you're getting!"

Ruth had taken her plate to the glider swing in the corner of the yard and was planning what to say to Joan—three minutes wasn't a whole lot of time when you hadn't seen each other in nearly ten days. She looked up to see their next-door neighbor, Mrs. Buell, beaming at her from the other side of one of the fat snowberry bushes that separated the two yards.

"I don't suppose I could interest anyone over there in a cupcake, could I?" Mrs. Buell inquired in her twinkly way. "I've got some extras I'd hate to let go stale. Some have vanilla icing and some have orange."

Ruth set her empty plate down and scrambled out of the swing. Mrs. Buell was always baking something delicious, in spite of food rationing; Ruth's mother said she must use all her butter and sugar just on desserts. Of course, there were only the two of them, now that their son Jack was in the Army.

Besides, it was always interesting to go into the Buells' yard, so much smaller and tidier than her own—a rectangle of thick, perfect grass with a hole in the middle for the clothesline tree and a rock garden on the far side that enclosed an oval goldfish pond.

While Mrs. Buell was in the kitchen, Ruth inspected the dark surface of the pond. She was relieved to see a flicker of orange in its depths. For a while, the Buells had kept a pair of little alligators instead of goldfish. Or maybe the alligators had eaten the goldfish—Ruth had never felt like asking. Betsy had been fascinated by the alligators, but Ruth thought they were creepy, even after she'd forced herself to touch one and had had to agree with Betsy that they weren't slimy.

She wondered what the Buells had done with them. *The New York Herald Tribune* said some people flushed their pet alligators down the toilet when they got tired of them. That was so disgusting

Ruth didn't even like to think about it. Also, what if the alligators didn't die but kept on growing down in the pipes somewhere?

"Here we are, dear." Mrs. Buell came down the cement step from the kitchen door with a pretty china plate. On it were eight cupcakes in pleated wrappers—four white ones and four orange, Ruth saw in some dismay. She foresaw a fight with her sisters over who got to have two orange cupcakes, assuming her parents took white ones and the girls were allowed to have seconds.

"Fred says to say hello," Mrs. Buell said, referring to her husband, a small, walnut-skinned man who ran a hardware store in a neighboring town. Mr. Buell was also the air-raid warden for their block, doing his rounds in a helmet that came down over his ears and made him look exactly like a picture-book gnome wearing a toadstool hat. Ruth and her sisters never giggled when they saw him, though—they were much too fond of him for that.

"He's got his feet up, listening to the radio," Mrs. Buell explained. "Feeling the heat, I expect."

For a moment, her kindly, soft features seemed to pucker. Ruth hadn't thought it was especially hot, not now at the end of the day, with the sun just a golden shimmer through the trees. Maybe Mrs. Buell didn't either, because she added with a sigh, "And of course he worries about Jack. He's on his way to the Pacific now, we think."

Ruth looked at her in alarm. "I thought Jack was at that camp, down in . . . in . . ."

"Georgia," Mrs. Buell supplied with a nod. "Well, he was, dear, but that was just for training, you know. They don't keep them there very long these days, I'm afraid. We hoped he might get a few days' leave, but . . ."

She shrugged her plump shoulders under her flower-sprigged housedress. "It does seem hard that they can't say where they're going. But then, I don't suppose they know themselves until the last minute."

She gazed down at the plate of cupcakes for a moment, then blinked and smiled, handing it to Ruth. "Well, now, you run along, dear, and give your family our love."

Ruth thanked her and went slowly back into her own yard. A ripe snowberry popped under her heel, but the sensation didn't give her its usual pleasure.

Jack Buell had always been an important person in her life—a lanky, slow-moving boy who towered over his parents and who always had a smile and a humorous word of greeting for the three little Owen girls next door. Secretly, Ruth had thought of him as a kind of older brother, someone she'd get to know better when she grew up.

Until now, she'd pictured Jack's being in the Army in terms of the cartoons in *The Saturday Evening Post* and songs on the radio like "You're in the Army, Mr. Jones" and "Oh, How I Hate to Get Up in the Morning"—that one especially, since Mr. Buell used to grumble that it practically took a cannon to get Jack out of bed on a school morning.

But now it seemed that instead of worrying about pulling his blanket so tight a mean-looking sergeant could bounce a coin on it, or getting his boots so shiny the same sergeant could see his face in them, Jack might be worrying about a torpedo hitting the ship he was on. And if that didn't happen, he'd have to worry about landing on some little island where sneaky Japanese soldiers would shoot at him from behind palm trees.

"Oh, how nice of Mrs. Buell," her mother said as Ruth set the plate of cupcakes on the round metal table her father repainted white each spring.

Instantly, Betsy dropped the paddle and ball she'd been playing with, trying to see if she could hit to a hundred without missing, and said, "Dibs on orange icing for firsts and seconds."

"No fair," Ruth protested, coming back to herself. "I was the one who brought them!"

Their father sighed. "Pick a number between one and thirty."

"Seven," said Carol in her funny, gruff voice, looking up from the doll she was undressing, its arms twisted backward over its head.

"You always say seven," Betsy told her scornfully. "And Daddy hasn't even had time to think of the number yet."

As Carol's face fell, Mrs. Owen said firmly, "One cupcake each is enough for now. We've all had plenty to eat. Don't argue, Betsy. We'll put the rest in the icebox and have them tomorrow. I hope you remembered to say thank you to Mrs. Buell, Ruth."

Ruth nodded. While they ate their cupcakes, she told them about Jack. Both her parents were silent for a moment. Then her father crumpled up his cupcake wrapper, tossed it into the trash can beside the table, and said, "Well, now, who's going to help me find a four-leaf clover? We haven't looked over by the jungle gym in a long time, and I bet there's at least one there."

"To bring Jack good luck," Carol said with a nod, setting her doll aside. "If we find one, we can send it to him. In a nenvelope, with a red stamp."

"*Envelope*, dummy," Betsy said, but added, "Yes, could we do that, Daddy?" as she followed her father over to the small wooden jungle gym at the rear of the yard.

"I don't see why not," Mr. Owen said. He took off his glasses and stretched out on the grass, propping his chin in his hands. He loved looking for four-leaf clovers and usually found one. This was partly because it was one of the few things he was patient about. It was also because he was so nearsighted that he could see small, close-up things very clearly. He didn't paw the grass the way most people did, just searched it methodically with his eyes.

Ruth lingered by the table, eyeing the remaining cupcakes and wondering if there was any more potato salad in the kitchen. She was still hungry. Even though she was skinny and small for her age, Ruth was always the first to clean her plate, and always felt that she never got quite enough to eat.

Her father was the same way. Sometimes they

met in the kitchen at night, looking into the icebox for something to nibble on. He would shake his head at her because of her mother's rule about not eating between meals, but if he was making a cheese sandwich for himself, usually he'd give Ruth a corner of it.

Ruth hoped she'd never be as nearsighted as her father, though, even if it meant she'd be good at finding four-leaf clovers. Maybe she couldn't quite read the blackboard from the back row, but at least she could tell a cow from a horse through a train window, which was more than her father could without his glasses.

CHAPTER

~~~~~~~~~~~~~~~~~~~~~~~~~~~~~~~~~~~~~~

FOUR

Thinking of this, she turned to her mother and said, keeping her voice low so her father wouldn't hear, "Do you think Daddy still minds about not being in the Navy?"

He'd been offered a commission, she knew—although she didn't know what a commission was, exactly—but then had been turned down because of his eyesight.

Mrs. Owen was gathering up glasses and silverware to take back to the kitchen. She hesitated, looking down at the cluster of forks she held in one hand, and said, "Yes, I'm afraid he does. He'd like to feel he was doing his part."

It was rare for her mother to look troubled or uncertain, but Ruth thought she did now, for just a moment.

Then she squared her shoulders and said briskly, "Of course, he wouldn't have been *in* the war, dear, just working in an office, pretty much the way he does now." Mr. Owen was an engineer who made plans for machines and electrical systems.

"And we would have had to move to Washington, D.C.," Ruth said, remembering the discussions she'd overheard.

"Well, maybe. It's terribly crowded there these days, and we might have had trouble finding a place to live. Probably Daddy would have stayed in a hotel and just come home on weekends whenever he could."

"You mean he wouldn't really live with us anymore?" Ruth stared at her mother in consternation. "I'm glad the Navy wouldn't let him in, then."

Her mother gave her shoulders a squeeze. That was unusual, too. Mostly it was Betsy and Carol she hugged, as if Ruth, being the oldest, didn't need to be hugged as often. "So am I, to be honest. A lot of other families aren't so lucky, you know. . . . Well, now, if you're not going to join the clover hunt, you can give me a hand with these things and then"—she looked at her small gold wristwatch, last year's Christmas present from all of them—"it'll be just about time to make your call to Joan."

Ruth helped her carry the trash can over to its place against the garage wall.

She said, "I think it's dumb, though, if the Navy turned Daddy down just because he has to wear glasses. If he was only going to be in an office, not on a ship or anything, what difference would being nearsighted make?"

Did wearing glasses mean you got left out of things somehow, as if other people assumed you weren't as strong or quick or capable as they were? That was what Ruth really wanted to ask, but she knew her mother wouldn't understand the question. If your eyesight needed fixing, you wore glasses and were grateful to have them, and that was that. You certainly didn't fuss about how they made you look. After all, you were still the same person underneath, weren't you?

"Oh, it's just one of their rules," Mrs. Owen said as they went in the back door. "The way the Army won't take people with flat feet, even if they're going to be cooks or supply sergeants or something and probably never have to do any marching. Whew, it's hot in here! Turn on the fan, would you, Ruth?"

Ruth grinned in spite of herself. "'The Flat Foot Floogee with the Floy, Floy,'" she sang, switching on the fan that stood on the kitchen table and watching the petal-shaped blades whir into a figure eight and then vanish altogether in a silvery blur.

"Really, the nonsense that comes over the radio these days," her mother said, but she was smiling as she reached up into a cupboard and took down the egg timer.

"Now, Ruth, you're to talk for three minutes exactly, no more." She gave the little hourglass a shake so that all the fine sand settled in the bottom part. "When the operator connects you, you're to turn the timer over and keep an eye on the three-minute line there. Is that understood?"

Ruth nodded solemnly. As she went into the hall and pulled a chair up to the telephone table, she decided it might be a good idea to write down a list of all the things she wanted to tell Joan in three minutes—or rather in the minute and a half that would be her share. It wasn't only the cost of telephoning long distance, she knew, but also the fact that the call was just for fun, not a necessary one like the war posters said. "Is This Call Necessary?" they demanded in big, reproachful letters.

But although she and Joan had a good connection, with hardly any static, the call didn't turn out to be much fun, after all.

For one thing, Joan sounded almost surprised to find that it was Ruth on the phone, as if she'd forgotten all about their arrangement. For another, she was so full of all the things she was doing up at the lake that Ruth was barely able to get a word in edgewise.

With almost half their precious time used up, Ruth crumpled up the list she'd made and blurted out the most important item on it—her continuing dread of going into sixth grade in the fall.

"But remember how bored you were last year?" Joan said reasonably. "Mrs. Chapman had to give you a special reading list and make up extra arithmetic problems—either that or keep sending you out of the room on some dumb errand. And it would be worse next year, because now you already know all the stuff we'll be learning."

"I'd rather be bored and still be with all my friends," Ruth protested. "I don't even know any of those sixth-grade girls, except for Mary Jo Douglas, and you know what *she's* like."

Mary Jo lived on the next block. She had a loud voice and greasy hair and always tried to cheat when they played Beckon, saying she'd seen someone beckoning to her when she hadn't.

Joan said, "I know, but they won't all be that way. Anyhow, Ruth, I don't think you should worry so much about age. This girl I was telling you about, Ann Reeves, the one who has a pony and goes to private school—well, she's a year younger than us, but she's really fun. She reads a lot, like you do. In fact she likes a lot of the same books—*My Friend Flicka* and *Lassie Come Home* and *Swiss Family Robinson.* Oh, I forgot to say she's learning the recorder too, and sometimes we play duets."

She giggled. "The hardest part is finding a place to practice. Usually we go down in the boathouse where no one can hear us. Once we tried playing in the field where Ann's pony is, only he got spooked by the high notes. Ann says—"

"Listen, Joan, our three minutes are almost up," Ruth interrupted unhappily, watching the sand trickling silently, unstoppably, into the bottom of the timer.

"Already? Okay, I guess we better hang up, then."

"Next time it's your turn to call," Ruth reminded her. "Two weeks from tonight."

"Sure. Only maybe we should make it three weeks. We might be staying longer," Joan explained rapidly, "because of the polio scare. My parents think it's safer up here in the country, where there aren't any crowds, so they're going to see if we can have the cottage till the end of August."

The receiver felt cold and heavy in Ruth's hand as she replaced it in its black cradle—as cold and heavy as her heart. Now she wouldn't see Joan until September. Worse, it didn't sound as if Joan even cared, happy with her new friend Ann (whom Ruth decided she hated) and not really minding any more about their being separated at school.

They'd agreed they wouldn't let Ruth's being a grade ahead make any difference. They'd still eat their lunches together and walk each other home from school. On winter weekends they'd still go ice-skating and sledding together. As often as their mothers would allow, they'd still stay over at each other's houses on Saturday nights, sneaking on the radio to listen to *Your Hit Parade* long after they were supposed to be asleep.

Now Ruth wondered if things would really work out that way. She thought of Joan's sparkling dark eyes and smooth cap of black hair, her infectious laugh and quick, confident movements, and knew there were plenty of fifth-grade girls who'd jump at the chance to be Joan's best friend. Boys liked her, too—Joan was always one of the first to be chosen

35

for teams, and usually got the most valentines of anyone in their homeroom.

"Ruth?"

Carol was standing in the kitchen doorway, clutching her grubby doll. Ruth scowled at her. The worst thing about being the oldest was that someone was always following you around and watching what you did and listening in if they could.

"What?" she said, in her most forbidding voice.

"We found one. A four-leaf clover." Carol's brown eyes were shining. "*I* found it," she said proudly. "Daddy says that means I'm lucky."

Ruth looked at her cute little sister, whose chestnut curls were haloed by the late sunlight streaming through the kitchen window behind her.

"Yes," she said bitterly. "You probably are."

CHAPTER

~~~~~~~~~~~~~~~~~~~~

FIVE

Except for having to get dressed up and wear a hat that looked stupid on her, Ruth didn't mind the church part of Sunday morning too much. What she minded was Sunday school, especially in summer.

The rest of the year they were divided into regular classes, and sometimes it could be sort of interesting to learn about people like the Good Samaritan and the man who took up his bed and walked.

In summer, though, they were all herded together in the parish hall and made to sit at a long table furnished with coloring books and crayons and dumb follow-the-dot puzzles. Soon the littlest kids would get bored and restless, and since there were only two teachers in charge, Ruth—as one of the older girls—had to spend most of her time chasing small boys around the room and dragging them back to their chairs.

This morning, sitting with her sisters at the end of a pew where they could be excused quietly before the sermon, Ruth viewed this prospect even more darkly than usual. Last night's conversation with Joan still rankled. Besides that, her parents had decided against going to the beach again today. It was Communion Sunday, which meant the service would be longer than usual. By the time they got home and changed, her father said, there'd be a lot of traffic heading for the beach—to say nothing of crowds when they got there, what with all the buses carrying people out of the hot city.

Ruth had heard on the radio that the temperature in New York City was supposed to get up to one hundred degrees today. The radio announcer also said the police were going to arrest anyone they caught turning on a fire hydrant, because the water might be needed to put out a fire. Ruth had seen city kids playing in the gush of rusty-looking water from the hydrants and thought it looked like fun— much more fun than just going under the garden hose, except maybe for all the icky stuff that might be floating in the gutter.

Here inside the tall, gray Episcopal church, though, the air felt almost shivery, with heavy blocks of stone walling off the outside air and colored windows filtering out the sun. Ruth shifted uncomfortably on the thin pew cushion and tugged at the waistband of her second-best summer dress, which was too tight under the arms.

At least that proved she'd grown some since last year. Unfortunately, Betsy had grown, too, meaning she couldn't always wear Ruth's hand-me-downs anymore. In fact, it was Betsy who'd gotten to have a new dress this summer, instead of Ruth— buttercup yellow, with crisp little tucks down the front and a floppy white collar. Ruth eyed it enviously, though the dress probably would have looked dumb on her.

Even her hand-me-downs usually looked better on Betsy than they had on Ruth, making her wonder if it was really Betsy her mother had in mind when they went shopping at Loeser's or Arnold Constable. This blue, for instance, was exactly the color of Betsy's eyes. Too bad she'd gotten too big to wear it, Ruth thought meanly.

The minister had climbed into the pulpit and was reading out some announcements. Ruth found herself thinking about Joan again—how Joan's clothes always fitted her perfectly and looked exactly right. Her red plaid skirt with the knife pleats, for instance, and her new penny loafers. Ruth's mother wouldn't let her have loafers. She said they were bad for her feet, so Ruth was still stuck with lace-up brown oxfords.

Of course, Joan was an only child, and the Deckers were richer than the Owens. For a long time Ruth had thought that was because their money just had to be divided among three people instead of five. Gradually, though, she'd understood that things like Mrs. Decker's fur coat and their big Buick and the new Frigidaire that made ice cubes in little trays cost a lot of extra money—more than her own parents would have been able to afford, even without Betsy and Carol to feed and buy clothes and shoes for.

The Deckers had a maid as well—Nora, a tall, rawboned woman who always seemed to be ironing something and who smelled, not unpleasantly, of blueing and starch. Last winter Ruth had heard Dr. Decker grumbling about having to pay Nora more money to stop her from going off to do war work in a factory. In the end, though, he must have paid it because Nora was still with them. Dr. Decker was a dentist, not an ordinary dentist, but the kind that straightened people's teeth.

Ruth's family might have been rich, too, at least on her mother's side, if it hadn't been for the Crash that had happened a few years before Ruth was born. (Ruth pictured this as a kind of earthquake that toppled people's best china off even the highest, safest shelves, though she knew it really had to do with something called the stock market.) Grandfather Prescott had had to close the doors of his bank, and by the time he paid everyone what the bank owed them, there was hardly any money left for him and Grandmother.

Now, instead of living in the big stone house in Brooklyn Heights where Ruth's mother and brothers had grown up, they lived in a three-room apartment crowded with dark furniture, and cooked their meals on a hot plate—or rather heated up food from cans, because Grandmother had never really learned to cook.

More bad luck, Ruth thought moodily. She'd been thinking a lot about luck recently. Not that her grandparents seemed particularly cast down. On the contrary, they joked about bumping their shins on the sideboard and having to go single file in the hallway because of the bookshelves on either side. When Ruth went to visit, they played Chinese checkers and always had a good dessert from the bakery around the corner—cream puffs or chocolate eclairs. Also, it was fascinating to explore her grandfather's closet, filled with smooth, dark suits and hand-stitched shoes that had been made for him in England. He still kept the shoes polished, too.

Maybe it made a difference that the Crash had been a lot of people's bad luck, Ruth thought. Like the war now, and the polio epidemic.

The minister had finished his announcements and was leading them in a special prayer for their fighting men overseas, reading out the names of all the sons and brothers and husbands. From her kneeling position, Ruth found herself thinking suddenly of what Joan had said about crowds. Did that mean it wasn't just swimming pool crowds you could get polio from, but any kind of crowd?

She sneaked an uneasy look at the bowed heads and shoulders around her. The congregation was a small one on this summer Sunday, but maybe it was big enough to be called a crowd. It was hard to imagine a polio germ lurking here among all these sober, well-dressed people. But if you could get a cold from someone like dignified old Mr. Murray, now blowing his nose loudly into a snowy handkerchief, maybe you could get polio, too.

Would her own parents have taken them to the country this summer if they could have afforded it?

The organ thundered out the opening bars of a hymn, and there was a rustle as the congregation rose to its feet.

"Eternal Father, strong to save, Whose arm hath bound the restless wave . . ." The hymn was one of Ruth's favorites because it was about the ocean. Although she wasn't musical like Joan, who played the piano as well as the recorder, she sang the words out heartily:

"O hear us when we cry to thee
For those in peril on the sea."

Ruth frowned down at the hymnal she was sharing with Betsy and almost lost her place. Until today, she'd pictured those in peril as reckless swimmers who'd gone out beyond the breakers on a rough day, or else as old-time sailors in striped jerseys pulling at the oars of a pitching boat with a tattered sail.

But all at once the picture in her mind was of Jack Buell in his soldier's uniform, standing at the rail of a gray battleship in a crowd of other soldiers. They were looking back at the land—at America and the houses they'd grown up in, with their parents standing on the front steps and the grass growing tall and thick in the yards they used to mow every Saturday afternoon.

As Ruth watched, or seemed to watch, the soldiers got smaller and smaller in the distance, until they were just tiny matchstick figures caught between the enormous sky and the endless, rolling miles of waves.

Looking at the faces of the adults around her, at the somber profiles of her own parents as they sang, Ruth understood for the first time that it was the war they were thinking about. That was why they were always singing this hymn lately—because of the war and its peril.

Betsy was nudging her. "Go on, Ruth," she whispered. "It's time!"

Ruth blinked, returning to herself with a start. The hymn had ended, and the minister was clearing his throat, ready to begin his sermon. Hastily she scrambled out of the pew, ducked her head toward the altar as she'd been taught, and led her sisters down the aisle to the tall, carved doors and the shimmer of the August day beyond.

CHAPTER

~~~~~~~~~~~~~~~~~~~~~~~~

SIX

One good thing about Sunday school—at least Ruth got to take off her hat.

She and her sisters wore identical Scotch caps with jaunty, peaked crowns and grosgrain ribbons hanging down the back, a gift from their Owen grandmother in Ohio. Their mother's friends were always saying how darling the three little girls looked in their matching hats, but Ruth knew it was Betsy and Carol who looked darling. The perky shape of the hat was all wrong for the shape of her own face, making it look even narrower and thinner than usual. Somehow it made her hair look straighter, too.

But actually, Sunday school turned out to be almost fun today, thanks to the heat. It was so stifling in the low-roofed parish hall, even with all

44

the windows open, that after about ten minutes, Mrs. Morgan and Mrs. Graham decided to let them go outside and play on the side lawn of the church.

"*Quietly*, though, children," Mrs. Graham cautioned in the doorway, holding a finger to her lips in her silly way. "We don't want to disturb the service. Now who can think of a nice, quiet game we can all play?"

Ruth sorted rapidly through a mental list of possibilities—she was used to organizing games for her sisters and the other kids in the neighborhood. "How about Green Light?" she suggested.

"Or Giant Steps," said a large, freckle-faced girl Ruth had never seen before. She had thick blond braids that reached below her shoulder blades, and wore a ruffled, pink-checked dress that looked too young for her. But maybe that was just because she was so tall—as tall as a junior-high girl, with big hands and feet.

Mrs. Graham beamed at both of them. "Very good, Ruth and—Laura, isn't it? Yes, Laura King, whose family has just moved to town. And this is her brother, Billy." She indicated a stocky, towheaded boy standing off to one side with his hands in his pockets and a sulky look on his face. "I'm sure we'll all do our best to make them feel welcome."

She turned back to Ruth and said distractedly, "Now, let me see, dear, I suppose we'll need someone to be 'it' . . ."

Some of the little boys were already tussling on the lawn, getting grass stains on their good pants.

Ruth said quickly, "Maybe we should divide into two groups. One group could play Green Light, and the other could go over on the other side of those trees and play Giant Steps." She turned to Mrs. Morgan, whom she considered the more sensible of the two women, and explained, "I could start out being 'it' with one group and she—Laura—could take the other."

"How come Ruth gets to be 'it'?" Betsy grumbled as Mrs. Morgan began counting them off into two groups.

"Yeah, and how come Laura does?" demanded the towheaded boy.

Ruth met Laura's eye; they shrugged and smiled at each other.

"Because it was their idea," Mrs. Morgan said briskly. "And anyway, isn't the whole point of the game to *keep* from being 'it'?"

Well, it was and it wasn't, Ruth thought, but you couldn't explain that to a grown-up.

The games weren't as quiet as they might have been, mainly because of a tendency to squeal whenever the person who was "it" got tagged and gave chase to the others. But at least there weren't any fights, and when it was time for juice and crackers in the shade of one of the big elm trees, everyone lined up in an orderly fashion.

Standing at the back of the line, Ruth got talking to Laura King and found out she came from

Nebraska and was in sixth grade, too. Not only that, she was going to be in Miss Amory's homeroom, like Ruth. The other sixth-grade teacher was grouchy old Mr. Burnside, who was always confiscating things and was said to have a locked drawer in his desk crammed full of marbles and slingshots and comic books and hundreds of bubble-gum wrappers.

"I'm really supposed to be in fifth," Ruth told Laura, her mood darkening again, "but I got skipped. They do that quite a lot here."

"Do they keep people back, too?" Laura sounded so eager that Ruth gave her a puzzled look. "I just thought if they did, maybe I wouldn't be the tallest one in the class, for once."

Ruth was so used to being short and skinny that she'd never really imagined what it must feel like to be so big for your age that you towered over all your classmates. Thinking of this, she said, "Well, at least you don't have to wear glasses." It was Laura's turn to look puzzled. "I'm probably going to have to," Ruth explained with a scowl. "I'm nearsighted."

"So is my brother." Laura sighed. "Only he hardly ever wears his glasses. Either he breaks them, accidentally on purpose, or he pretends he's lost them. My mom gets really mad at him. She didn't make him wear them today, though, because of being new."

Ruth thought Laura's mother sounded very understanding. She also thought that maybe she herself could get away with wearing her glasses only part of the time. Of course, she wouldn't break them—glasses cost a lot, she knew—but there was nothing that said she had to wear them after school, or even at recess.

This was such a cheering thought that she was surprised to find Laura still looking downcast.

"Billy really hates it here," she said. "He misses the sky."

"The sky?" Ruth looked up at the vivid patches of summer blue tangled in the leaves of the elm tree.

"It's not *big* here, like it is at home." Laura swept her arms wide to demonstrate. Mrs. Graham was just reaching over Ruth's shoulder to hand Laura a little paper cup of apple juice, and Laura almost knocked her hat off. She mumbled an apology, flushing under her freckles.

"I'm always doing clumsy things like that," she muttered as she and Ruth took their juice and crackers around to the other side of the tree.

Ruth was thinking maybe she understood what Laura meant about the sky. It was something she loved about the beach—that feeling of being able to see as far as you could in all directions. "If you like a whole lot of sky," she said, "you should go to the ocean. To Jones Beach—that's where my family always goes."

"I've never even seen the ocean, except in the movies," Laura confessed, brightening a little. "It looks like it would be scary to go swimming in, but fun." Her face fell again. "But that wouldn't be the same, though—a place you have to drive to. At home, you just walk out the back door, and there's the prairie and the sky going on forever and ever. You know, like in the song—'amber waves of grain.'"

It didn't sound very exciting to Ruth, but then, she'd only seen pictures of the prairie, just as Laura had only seen pictures of the ocean. She nodded politely.

"I think it's sort of pretty here," Laura conceded, "with all the trees and the green grass and the houses being so close together and everything, but Billy . . . well, he feels sort of cooped up. He wants to be a farmer when he grows up. All my dad's brothers are farmers," Laura explained, "and my granddad, too. We've always lived on my grand-parents' farm, even though my dad's an engineer and had to drive to Omaha every day. But now he has a new job at Sperry, on account of the war, so we had to move here."

Ruth was about to say that her father was an engineer, too, when Laura's brother Billy, crossing the lawn with another boy, came to a sudden halt and burst out laughing.

"Boy, do you two look funny together," he said, pointing at Laura and Ruth. "Like Mutt and Jeff in the funny papers." He punched the other boy in the arm, and they both doubled over. Some of the other kids looked around to see what the joke was.

"Shut up, Billy," Laura said angrily. As he ran off, still laughing, she said to Ruth, "My brother can be a real dope sometimes. And I was just feeling sorry for him!"

Ruth glared at Betsy and Carol, who'd been giggling, too. "You must really hate having a younger brother," she said, trying not to notice that the top of her head only came up to Laura's shoulder. "Sometimes I can't stand my little sisters, either. I've decided what I'd really like to have is an older brother. Either that or be an only child."

"I don't know." Laura looked thoughtful. "Only children can be really spoiled. I have a baby brother at home," she added, "and he's just as cute as can be. Sometimes I get to give him his pabulum and look after him when my mom's busy."

Pabulum—ugh! Ruth could still remember how Carol used to smear it all over her face, even on her eyebrows, and then bang her spoon on the tray of her high chair so everyone would look at her and laugh. When Carol misbehaved, her parents thought she was cute. When Ruth misbehaved, she got sent to her room.

Ruth heard organ music and looked over at the church. People were filing out of the big doors, shaking the minister's hand and stopping to chat on the steps while they fanned themselves with their programs.

A few minutes ago, Ruth had been on the point of asking Laura where she lived and inviting her to go to the beach with them sometime. Now she hesitated, telling herself she ought to ask her mother first.

50

But it wasn't just that. She'd had a sudden dismaying picture of herself and Laura, two new sixth-grade girls, on the first day of school. If she made friends with Laura, it would be only natural for them to stick together, and what if people laughed? They probably *did* look pretty funny side by side, she thought, almost like members of different species. A horse, say, and a squirrel . . . worse, a squirrel wearing glasses.

Besides, no one Ruth knew thought babies were cute. No one wore their hair in braids, either, except for Hilda Gutterson, whose father spoke English with an accent and who some kids said was a German spy. Ruth thought Laura's braids were kind of pretty, not stiff like Hilda's but golden and shiny like cornsilk in the sunlight. Still—

"I see my mom looking for me," she told Laura quickly. "See you next week."

She tossed her paper cup into the wire basket beside the tree. Then, feeling the space between her shoulder blades begin to prickle with the lie, she hurried along the walk to the parish hall to retrieve her hated hat.

CHAPTER

~~~~~~~~~~~~~~~~~~

SEVEN

Ruth weighed down her towel against the wind with her sandals and her library book. The fourth corner still flapped, so she dumped some sand on it. Then she straightened, holding back the strands of hair blowing across her face, and squinted along the beach to see if Russ was in the lifeguard's chair today. But it was too far—she couldn't tell for sure.

"There's that nice lifeguard again," her mother said, answering the question for her. Ruth thought resignedly that she really did need glasses. "And there's another lifeguard with him. I'm glad to see they're doubling up today."

It hadn't seemed very windy at home, just a pleasant breeze ruffling the crowns of the maple trees along Kempton Road. But there'd been whitecaps on Great South Bay, and when they turned onto the beach road, they'd seen the flag that meant swimming would be restricted in some areas today.

Even though such restrictions didn't usually apply to Number Nine, where the sand shelved away very gradually and there weren't any dangerous currents, Mrs. Owen had slowed the car and almost turned back. Then Betsy pointed out that they had to eat their picnic lunch somewhere, and it might as well be at the beach. They wouldn't even have to go in the water, she said, if it was too rough.

Ruth, of course, planned to, whatever the water was like, though she'd had to promise her mother not to go in over her head without her father there. Mrs. Owen was a stylish swimmer, with a smooth Australian crawl, but she hadn't taken a course in lifesaving like Mr. Owen.

"Come on, Betsy," Ruth urged now, turning to face the ocean. "We'll hold hands and just jump the waves. Look, it's low tide now, and they aren't even very big."

Betsy eyed the choppy blue water while the wind flattened her curls against her head. "Maybe I'll go in later," she said. "Right now I want to go look for shells and crabs and things."

"Take me, Ruth!" Carol begged as Betsy set off along the hard sand at the water's edge, carrying a pail in which to store her finds. Ruth hoped she wouldn't bring back any dead fish. "Can Ruth take me in the water, Mommy?"

"Well, all right, but just wading," their mother said.

The tide was so low that Ruth barely got wet as she wandered around with Carol's hand in hers. Carol was delighted by all the shallow water, though, and said she wanted to practice her swimming. She had just learned the dog paddle.

Mindful of her promise, Ruth sent her back up onto the beach to get permission. Their mother was standing talking to a large woman wearing a flowered bathing suit and a white bandanna around her head. Carol had to tug her hand several times to get her attention. Mrs. Owen nodded distractedly, and Carol scampered back to where Ruth stood hugging herself against the breeze. She'd probably be warmer in the water than out of it.

"Now remember," Carol said, "you have to keep your hand under my tummy—not holding me up, but *touching*."

"Who's Mom talking to?" Ruth asked curiously.

"Oh, some lady she knows. She's friends with the Stewarts, only they're sick. They had to have the doctor come. Wait, I better get my face wet first."

Carol screwed up her eyes, bent over at the waist, and dipped her face in the water. As she raised it again, gasping and spitting, Ruth said, "Who had to have the doctor?"

The Stewarts were friends of their parents. They had three boys who were almost the same ages as Ruth and her sisters, and they were always inviting them to the boys' birthday parties.

"I don't know. Randy, I guess."

Carol said this with an air of satisfaction. She and Randy Stewart always fought when the two families got together, though Ruth herself liked him the best of the three boys. David, the one nearest her own age, was a handsome boy with an aloof, superior manner, polite but never really friendly. Ruth dreaded going to David's birthday parties, in spite of the fact that they'd had a magician once and always showed cartoons down in the basement rec room after the ice cream and cake—Mickey Mouse and Porky Pig and (Ruth's favorite) Felix the Cat.

"Come on, Ruth, I'm ready," Carol said. She was stretched out in the water, kicking her feet.

"No fair holding onto the bottom," Ruth told her, crouching down and turning her face away from Carol's splashing.

"I won't if you'll keep your hand under me, like Daddy does."

Ruth slid the flat of her hand under Carol's barrel-like stomach. Carol took a big breath, tensed her body, and paddled furiously for about five seconds. Then she looked over her shoulder and said disappointedly, "I didn't go anywhere. You were holding on!"

"No, I wasn't. You just forgot to kick."

In fact, Carol was so buoyant in the water, it would have been hard to hold her down. Ruth envied people who could float easily. She herself sank like a stone in fresh water. Even in salt water she couldn't float for more than half a minute without having to move her arms or legs. One of her ambitions was to go swimming in Great Salt Lake. She'd seen pictures of people bobbing around in the water there, reading newspapers.

This gave her an idea. "Listen, Carol, forget about using your arms. Just do the dead man's float—you know, with your hands straight out in front—and kick your feet. That way, you'll really move."

Carol disliked putting her face in the water for more than a few seconds, but finally Ruth persuaded her take a deep breath and try. Unfortunately, the tide was coming in, and just as Carol raised her head to get another breath, a small wave smacked her in the face. She swallowed water, spluttered, and started to cry.

"You're all right," Ruth told her encouragingly. "And look how far you went! Come on, try it again."

Carol shook her head. "I like it better the other way."

Ruth sighed. "Okay, but that's not really learning how to swim."

"It is, too! I bet that's how you learned."

But she looked up at her older sister uncertainly, her wet dark ringlets clinging to her cheeks. Actually, Ruth couldn't remember learning to swim, any more than she could remember learning to read. It seemed like something she'd always known how to do.

"All right," Carol said suddenly, to Ruth's

surprise. "I might try it one more time. Only you watch and tell me if there's a wave coming."

Ten minutes later, Carol was almost swimming—kicking and paddling with her face in the water, raising her head to suck in a noisy breath, then kicking and paddling some more.

"Okay," Ruth said at last. "That's enough of a lesson for now."

She needed to go for a swim herself before she got any colder. Besides, the strip of shallow water was shrinking by the moment, beginning to swirl with sand and foam and little shells.

To her relief, Carol didn't argue, only nodded solemnly. Then her face split into an enormous grin. She dashed up onto the beach, windmilling her arms and yelling, "Mommy! Mommy, did you see me? I was really swimming!"

CHAPTER

EIGHT

Smiling to herself, Ruth pushed forward into the waves. They were unexpectedly strong, and so choppy you couldn't really jump them or dive through them, let alone ride one in to shore. Remembering she wasn't supposed to go in over her head, she tried to stay where the water was only up to her chin. But the sand was bumpy and uneven under her feet, and the waves kept lifting her over hollows where she couldn't quite touch bottom.

Ruth turned and tried swimming parallel to the shore, using the overarm sidestroke her father had taught her, so she could keep an eye on the waves. It was hard going, though, with the water so churned up. After a long, bristly cord of seaweed wrapped itself around her wrist, Ruth gave up and let the waves push her back into shallow water.

"Hi, there, Ruth!"

Ruth looked up to see Russ waving at her from his tall, white chair. She'd swum farther up the beach than she'd realized. Russ was alone in the chair now, she was glad to see. She'd been hoping to talk to him again but had felt shy about approaching him when he was with another lifeguard.

As she scuffed through the warm, powdery sand, she saw the other lifeguard down by the high-tide line, leaning against the big rowboat they used for rescues. He was a grizzled older man with burly shoulders burned mahogany by the sun. Russ was more of a golden color, with a fuzz of blond hair on his arms and legs. Today he'd smeared a white triangle of sunburn cream over his nose, giving him a clownish look that made Ruth smile.

"I look like Emmett Kelly, don't I?" he called down.

Emmett Kelly was a famous clown with the Ringling Brothers Circus, Ruth knew, even though she'd never been to the circus. Her parents were waiting until Carol was old enough to appreciate it.

Sometimes it seemed to Ruth that she was always waiting to do things until her sisters got old enough. Joan had already been to the circus twice, and to the ballet *The Nutcracker Suite* at Christmastime. She was always getting to go to Radio City Music Hall, too, and not just to see baby movies like *Dumbo* and *Bambi*.

"Say, I saw you teaching your little sister to

swim," Russ said in his friendly way. "You must be a good teacher—she was really making progress."

"She can be a terrible crybaby sometimes," Ruth told him offhandedly, trying not to show how pleased she felt. "But I guess maybe she's starting to grow up a little."

"Give her time," Russ advised with a grin, returning his gaze to the ocean. "Speaking as the youngest of five kids, I can promise you it'll happen."

"Five kids!" That was a big family, like her parents said people used to have before the Crash. Ruth knew hardly any families that even had three children, like her own.

"Three sisters, one brother. It wasn't easy, I can tell you." Russ shook his head. "The mashed potatoes were always cold by the time they got passed to me, and I was just a tagalong when it came to playing Kick the Can or going to the candy store."

Ruth thought about this. Did Carol ever feel like a tagalong? It seemed to her that Carol got the most attention of anyone in the family, but maybe that was just because she needed taking care of the most. She also thought about Carol getting big, as big as Betsy. What if she, Ruth, ended up being the smallest sister in spite of being the oldest?

Russ glanced down at her. "Hey, you're covered with goose bumps. Have a towel." He tossed one down, a stiff white towel with an official-looking laundry mark on it. As Ruth rubbed her sticky, wet hair, he added, with that way he had of guessing her thoughts, "You know, you may be kind of small for your age now, but I bet you're going to shoot up one of these days and wind up being tall, like your dad."

That was what Ruth's mother was always saying, too. But it was right now that Ruth cared about.

She sat down on the sand with the towel around her shoulders and stared moodily at her skinny outstretched legs. After a while, drifting a handful of sand over one bony kneecap, she said, "Did you ever have to skip a grade in school?"

Russ laughed. "Me? Listen, I was lucky to get promoted from one year to the next. The only subject I was ever any good at was science."

"Like my sister Betsy," Ruth said, nodding. "She wants to be a doctor when she grows up."

"That right? So did I, until . . . when I was younger." Ruth looked up at him quickly, wondering what he'd been about to say. Until what? Until he found out he wasn't smart enough? But she couldn't tell anything from his profile, especially with all that silly white gunk on his nose.

"Either that or be an explorer," Russ went on, shifting his weight and crossing one ankle over the other. It must get uncomfortable sitting for so long, Ruth thought, even though the seat had a padded boat cushion on it. "I was going to hunt dinosaur bones in the desert, or maybe climb Mount Everest, just for fun." He gave a wry chuckle.

"Well, you still can," Ruth said. "I mean, you

won't always be a lifeguard, will you?" For the first time, she wondered what Russ did in the wintertime. Maybe he went to college, she thought. He seemed about the right age for that, a couple of years older than Jack Buell.

Russ didn't answer her question. Maybe he hadn't heard it. Instead he said, "Hey, see that sailboat there, the one drifting this way? Looks like it's in some kind of trouble." He picked up the big pair of binoculars he kept beside him on the seat.

Ruth had been watching a fat man in baggy red trunks trying to set up an oversized striped umbrella in the damp tidal sand below her. Meanwhile his wife and little boy had unfolded a pair of canvas deck chairs and were opening a large picnic hamper that had a whole set of silverware fitted cunningly into the underside of the lid. There was even a checked tablecloth which the wife started to unfold but stuffed hastily back in the hamper when the wind almost snatched it away.

Now Ruth transferred her gaze to the ocean, where she could see a scattering of white sails in the distance, all leaning at the same angle. The sailboat Russ must mean was closer to shore, though, closer than boats usually came, and it was moving oddly. One moment it would tip way over, so the sail almost touched the water. The next moment, the mast would be upright again, with the sail flapping in the wind. Ruth could make out someone moving around on deck, but she couldn't see if there was more than one person on board.

"Right, we'd better lend a hand," Russ decided, and blew a short blast on his whistle.

Down by the rowboat, the other lifeguard looked around, nodded, and motioned to a couple of boys playing catch nearby to help him push the heavy boat into the water. In seconds, it seemed, he'd buckled on his orange life jacket, scrambled aboard, and started rowing strongly toward the struggling sailboat.

"A job after Pete's heart," Russ said with a grin. "He'd give his eyeteeth to join the Coast Guard, but they turned him down—too old."

He studied the sailboat again through his binoculars. "Probably just a fouled rudder from all the seaweed," he said, and lowered the glasses. "That's tough to handle if you're alone, though. Well, now"—he relaxed and sat back, glancing down at Ruth—"what was all that about skipping a grade? Hey, I guess you're even smarter than I thought."

Ruth had stood up to get a better view. A lot of other people on the beach were standing too, shading their eyes to look out to sea, the way they always did when the lifeboat went out. When she didn't say anything, Russ dropped his teasing tone and said, "You don't seem too happy about it."

"They never even asked me if I wanted to," Ruth muttered, twisting the ends of the towel between her fingers.

"Who didn't ask you? Your parents?"

"My parents, and the principal, and the lady at

school who gave me a lot of tests. They just told me I'd be going into sixth grade instead of fifth next year. They expected me to be glad about it, but I'm not." Ruth swallowed over the lump that had risen in her throat. "I'll always be younger than everyone else in my class, and I'll never fit in."

"Sure you will," Russ told her. "Listen, Ruth, I'm pretty sure they don't skip people just because they're smart. They look at other things, too, like how well you get along with other kids and whether you're a leader and—" He broke off suddenly. "Watch it!"

Ruth had half-turned to look up at Russ. She turned back just in time to dodge the spokes of the big, striped umbrella, which had pulled out of the sand and was being blown up the beach by the wind.

It bumped past her like a giant tumbleweed, picked up speed, and started to cartwheel. Ruth ran after it and managed to grab the center pole before the umbrella smashed into a pair of sunbathers lying prone on the sand. It was surprisingly heavy, even after she'd dragged it around to face the wind.

"Thanks, girlie." The fat man came puffing up, red-faced. "Thought I finally had it in deep enough, but this blasted wind. . . . Brand-new umbrella, too—hope nothing got busted."

Ruth took the end of the pole and helped him carry the umbrella back down toward the water.

As they passed the lifeguard's chair, Russ looked down and said sharply, "You're lucky that didn't hurt someone, mister." In a milder voice, he added,

"You'll do better with it up this way, where the sand's drier. Besides, the tide's coming in."

The fat man followed his glance and saw that the water was already lapping at one of the folding chairs, unnoticed by his wife and son, who were watching the boats. His face went even redder. He muttered something under his breath and changed direction, plodding off to one side with the umbrella and dragging Ruth with him. She hung on to her end, feeling the wind tug at the striped canvas.

"Husky young fella like that," the man said, stabbing the pole into the sand. "Why isn't he in uniform, I'd like to know?" He scowled over his shoulder at Russ, then yelled at his wife to start moving their things. "Can't you see the tide's coming in?"

The sailboat was moving freely now, skimming away to join the other white sails on the horizon. Ruth looked from it to Russ, who was watching the lifeboat maneuver back through the choppy waves.

"He's doing an important job," she said with a frown. "Just as important as being in the Army or Navy."

"A nice, safe job, anyway," the man said with a grunt. "High and dry in that chair of his. Didn't even take the lifeboat out himself, you notice—just sent the old guy to do the dirty work."

Ruth started to say that Pete had been down by the boat in the first place, and also that he liked taking it out. But the fat man was already trudging away from her, yelling to his son to grab his shoes before a wave got them.

Had Russ heard what he'd said? Ruth didn't think so. Still, she felt awkward somehow. As she retraced her steps, she saw the towel he'd lent her lying on the sand behind the chair. It must have slipped from her shoulders when she ran after the umbrella.

She hesitated, looking up at Russ's head and shoulders outlined against the sky. She didn't really feel like going back to the conversation they'd been having before. Why had she gotten started talking about school, anyway? That was the last thing she needed to think about on this breezy, blue beach day, when it was still summer, when nothing really bad could happen to her for at least a few more weeks. Besides, the way her stomach was growling, it must be almost lunchtime.

Quickly, Ruth picked up the towel, shook it out, and hung it over a back rung of the chair. As she broke into a trot, heading back to her family down the beach, she gave Russ a wave over her shoulder. But she didn't know if he saw.

CHAPTER

~~~~~~~~~~~~~~~~~~~~~~~~~~~~

NINE

Dear Joan,

I was glad to get your letter. It sounds neat there with canoes and horseback riding and everything. What color pony is Peanuts? Mom took us to see the movie *Lassie Come Home.* It was super! There's a girl in it named Elizabeth Taylor. I'm going to send away for her picture.

We've been going to the beach quite a lot, but today it's raining and also everything is sad here. Do you remember Alan Selby down the street? He used to set off firecrackers to scare the Fosters' dog. One time he dared Betsy to climb a big tree and when she couldn't get back down he just laughed and went away.

Well, he got killed in the war, over in Italy. At first they said he was Missing in Action, but now they know he's dead. The Selbys have a gold star in the window and they keep their blackout shades down in the daytime. It's hard to believe. I know I never liked Alan very much, but still.

The other sad thing is that a family we know got polio, all three boys. You met the oldest one at my birthday party, David Stewart. He had it the worst and almost died because he couldn't breathe, but now he's all right. The middle boy whose name is Jonathan was really sick too, but he's home now and they think he'll be able to walk okay, only with a limp. But the littlest one, Randy—

Ruth put down her fountain pen and stared at the windowpane, where drops of rain were sliding down like tears. Her mother had talked to Mrs. Stewart on the phone this morning, and when she hung up she couldn't speak. She'd put her arms around Ruth and her sisters and held them pressed against her like that for what seemed like a long time. Then she'd tied a scarf around her head and gone out for a walk, even though it was raining.

—Randy is still in the hospital and he'll probably have to stay there until

Thanksgiving at least. His legs won't move at all. They think he'll have to be in a wheelchair till his arms get strong enough so he can use crutches. I guess the braces they put on are really heavy.

Well, I'm sorry this is such a sad letter but that's the way things are right now. Maybe it won't seem so sad up in New Hampshire with all the fun you're having. Don't forget to call me a week from Saturday. By then I'll probably have some better things to tell you.

Love, Ruth

Ruth read the letter over and gave a sigh. It certainly wasn't anything like Joan's letter, which had been full of jokes and funny drawings. She had also enclosed a snapshot of her and her friend Ann standing on a narrow wooden dock. Ann was as tall as Joan, even though she was younger, with straight blond hair and what Ruth had to admit was a nice smile.

Maybe she could add a P.S. about how she'd made friends with one of the lifeguards at Number Nine, and how he was really nice, not mean and bossy the way they'd always thought lifeguards had to be.

But Ruth had been feeling uneasy about Russ. In spite of what she'd said to the fat man, was it really fair that Russ got to stay out of the war, when so many other boys and young men had to go and get shot at and maybe even killed, like Alan?

Of course, Russ might have tried to join and been turned down, like her father. But there was nothing wrong with his eyesight, Ruth knew. She didn't think he had flat feet, either. Russ's feet were at her eye level when she stood beside the lifeguard chair, so she could picture them clearly—high-arched and strong-looking, with short, straight toes.

Or she could tell Joan about the new girl, Laura. But that might sound as if Laura was her friend, and Ruth was guiltily aware that she hadn't done anything about inviting Laura over. She hadn't even talked to her again in a friendly kind of way. Yesterday at Sunday school, she'd sat at the opposite end of the long table from Laura and only said "hi" to her quickly when they were getting in line for refreshments. Then one of the little boys had spilled his juice, which gave Ruth an excuse not to say anything else while she went to get a dishrag.

"What're you doing?" Betsy appeared in the doorway of Ruth's room, looking bored and out-of-sorts.

"What does it look like I'm doing?" Carefully, Ruth printed Joan's address on an envelope.

Betsy and Carol shared a room at the other end of the hall, bigger and lighter than her own. Still, Ruth was glad she had a room to herself. It was one of the few good things about being the oldest.

"I was playing pickup sticks with Carol," Betsy

said sulkily, "but she isn't any good at it. The only ones she can pick up are the ones that are already loose. Now she's lying on her bed, pretending to read. I said I'd read to her from *The Five Little Peppers And How They Grew,* but she didn't even want to do that. She says she has a sore throat."

They looked at each other. "Did Mom take her temperature?" Ruth asked.

"Yes, and she doesn't have any fever, or a stiff neck or anything. Mom thinks it's just a cold, or maybe her tonsils."

Ruth and Betsy had had their tonsils out two years ago. That was the one time they'd shared a room, with Carol's crib moved into Ruth's room. It had been kind of fun, once their throats stopped hurting so much. They'd gotten to eat a lot of orange ice and listen to serials on the radio, like *Our Gal Sunday* and *Young Doctor Malone* and *Mary Noble, Backstage Wife.*

The hospital part of it was only a blur in Ruth's memory, except for the smells and the squeak of the nurses' rubber-soled shoes on the linoleum floors. She thought of little Randy Stewart lying in one of those beds with rails around it, like a cage, looking up at the ceiling and trying not to cry. Once when they were having a snowball fight in the vacant lot down the street, Carol had thrown a chunk of ice at Randy and cut his forehead open, but he hadn't cried, even though it must have hurt a lot.

Ruth hated the way polio was making everything so scary. The minute Betsy'd said that about Carol's sore throat, Ruth had found herself trying to remember if they'd been in any crowds lately. All she could think of was going to the movies in Hempstead, but their mother had taken them to the late-morning show, and there'd been hardly anyone else in the theater.

"Anyway," Betsy said, "now I don't have anything to do." She'd been wandering restlessly around the room. Suddenly she came to a halt in front of Ruth's bureau. "Those are my scissors!" she said, snatching them up.

"No, they're not," Ruth said automatically.

"Yes, they are. Here's my mark, see?" She showed Ruth a tiny red dot on one of the handles, made with their mother's nail polish.

Ruth could see her deciding whether to get really mad or not. Betsy was very possessive about her things, even dumb things like dried-up palm crosses left over from Palm Sunday and broken balsa-wood wings of model aiplanes. Their father said it came from being the middle child. Right now, though, Ruth could tell Betsy needed someone to do something with more than she needed to get mad.

Sure enough, she dropped the scissors into the pocket of her scruffy blue overalls—Ruth's old overalls, with the straps let out all the way—and said, "Do you want to play jacks?"

Ruth shook her head, though it was one of the few games she could usually beat Betsy at. "We can't, unless we put the puzzle away."

It was too wet to play jacks on the front porch, and the floor of the little sunroom they used as a playroom was covered by a large jigsaw puzzle they were all working on.

"We better not," Betsy decided. "Daddy said he might finish the sky part tonight."

Their father was almost as good at doing jigsaw puzzles as he was at finding four-leaf clovers. Thinking of this reminded Ruth of Jack Buell. As Carol had suggested, they'd sent Jack a clover, carefully pressed between two tiny pieces of cardboard, along with a card Ruth had bought at the ten-cent store with part of her allowance. It said "Wishing You the Best of Luck!" in fancy gold letters, and they'd all signed their names.

Ruth hoped the clover wouldn't dry out too much by the time Jack got it. The Buells didn't have a real address for him, just an Army box number. Although they wrote him every day, they knew he only got their letters in batches, the way they got his, usually several weeks after the date on the last one.

Ruth looked down at her own letter to Joan and decided to go mail it now at the box over on Spaulding Avenue. It was the middle of the afternoon, and Chip the mailman had long since come and gone. First, though, she needed to get a stamp from her mother.

"Can I come with you?" Betsy asked, trailing her down the stairs.

Ruth shrugged. "If you want. It's still raining, though."

"I'll get our slickers," Betsy offered. "We don't need our boots—we can just go barefoot."

Mrs. Owen was in the kitchen, slicing a banana into a glass bowl to mix with the raspberry Jell-O she was making. She glanced at the envelope in Ruth's hand and said, "Oh, Ruth, there was something else in the mail for you besides Joan's letter. A little envelope—I put it on the desk. It looks like an invitation."

Ruth frowned. She couldn't think of anyone she knew who had a birthday in August. She said, "Can I get a stamp, if you have any?"

"In the pigeonhole on the right." Her mother gave a stir to the saucepan and looked back at Ruth. "Oh, heavens, Ruth, look at your fingers! Get that ink off first, please. I hope it's the washable kind."

Ruth could never use a pen, even one that didn't leak, without getting ink all over her fingers. She thought it had something to do with being left-handed and trying to write straight up and down in the awkward way Mrs. Chapman had taught her, instead of curving her hand around the top of the paper. That was another thing that made her different in her family. Even her father was right-handed.

As she stood at the sink rinsing off the ink— Scripto's Washable Blue—and gazing at the can of Dutch cleanser with its fascinating repeating picture of the woman holding the can with a picture on it of the same woman holding the same can, and so on, her mother said, "When are the

Deckers coming back, do you know? I need to make an appointment for Betsy with Dr. Decker."

"Betsy?" Ruth turned to stare at her mother. "Betsy doesn't need to get her teeth straightened— she has the best teeth of any of us. I'm the one that needs braces, for my front teeth."

Mrs. Owen sighed. "Now, Ruth, we've been all through that. Dr. Wood says they'll get closer together as you grow older. And braces are terribly expensive, you know."

Dr. Wood was their regular dentist, the one who put fillings in.

"I don't really know how we're going to afford them for Betsy," her mother went on, pouring a thick red stream of Jell-O from the saucepan into the bowl, "but it seems her jaw is too small for the new teeth that are coming in, and something has to be done."

"I'm going to have to wear *braces*?" Betsy was standing in the dining room door, their yellow slickers bunched over her arm.

"That's not fair!" Ruth said in outrage.

"Who said?" Betsy demanded, and added, "I won't!"

"Now calm down, both of you. It's not definite yet, Betsy—we'll have to see what Dr. Decker says."

Mrs. Owen put the bowl of Jell-O in the icebox, took out a package wrapped in butcher paper, and closed the door hard. She got another bowl from the shelf and dumped the meat into it.

"Ugh, meat loaf *again*?" Betsy exclaimed, her teeth momentarily forgotten.

"Yes, meat loaf again, and you'd better be grateful for it! It's a lot more than most children get to eat in this world today. And yes, I could give you lamb chops for supper more often if I were willing to deal with a black-market butcher, like some of the women in this town."

Actually Ruth liked meat loaf, at least the way her mother made it, and thought having it so often was one of the few good things about the war.

"And as for wearing braces on your teeth, or not wearing them, if that's all you two have to worry about, I'd say you're pretty lucky."

This silenced even Betsy. Ruth could see her thinking about the other kind of braces, the ones Randy Stewart would have to wear on his crippled legs.

She also saw that her mother's hands were shaking as she opened a can of tomatoes. That was scary, somehow. It was one thing for Mom to get mad at them. It was another for her to be upset inside herself.

As Ruth went into the living room to get her stamp, she heard Betsy asking in a subdued voice if she could put the empty tomato can in the special press their father had made, to flatten it for the scrap collection. Mrs. Owen said all right, but to wash it out first and be sure not to cut herself. She still sounded cross.

CHAPTER

~~~~~~~~~~~~~~~~~~~~~~~~~~~~

TEN

After she'd put a stamp on her letter to Joan, Ruth opened the small envelope her mother had mentioned. It contained a folded invitation card with a silly-looking pink frog on the front and filled-in blanks on the inside giving the date, time, and place of the party. Under "place," beneath the address, it said "BRING YOUR BATHING SUIT!" in capital letters. The invitation was from a sixth-grade girl named Vickie Blair. Ruth knew who she was, but that was all.

"Oh, you lucky!" Betsy was looking over her shoulder. "That's Todd Blair's sister. They have a pool in their backyard—a real one, with a diving board and everything. Todd's always bragging about it."

When Ruth didn't say anything, she added

quickly, "It's okay to go in a pool like that, I'm pretty sure. It's not like a public pool."

"Why would she invite me?" Ruth said with a frown. "I don't even know her."

"I think Mom knows Mrs. Blair," Betsy said thoughtfully. "From playing tennis."

They both knew what that meant—an invitation arranged between mothers. Betsy wouldn't have minded, but Ruth did.

Slowly she put the card back in its envelope, already feeling a little sick to her stomach, even though the party wasn't until next Saturday. Unless she really got sick, she'd have to go. If she said she didn't want to, her mother would say firmly, "Now, Ruth, it'll be a good way to meet some of your new classmates before school starts," and Ruth wouldn't be able to argue with that.

"Is it a birthday party?" Betsy asked, handing Ruth her slicker. "Because if it is, you could get her one of those funny animals you blow up and ride around on in the water. That would be a neat present."

"I don't know," Ruth said heavily. "The invitation doesn't say."

"Well, you can ask Vickie when you call her up," Betsy said, opening the front door.

Ruth put on her slicker, slid Joan's letter into one of the big pockets, and followed Betsy out into the warm, rainy afternoon. Just the thought of calling someone she didn't know made her feel sick.

Betsy was brooding about her teeth again. "It's all backwards," she complained as they went down the walk. "You're the one that wants to get braces and I'm the one that doesn't. Why does everything have to be the wrong way around?"

The rain had made a stream in the gutter, a miniature river running the length of Kempton Road. Automatically they both stepped down from the curb to wade in it.

Ruth tried not to see that there were some yellow maple leaves swirling in the water along with the green ones, and even one leaf that had already turned orange. Instead she thought how every night for a whole month, after her parents had kissed her good night, she'd wound a rubber band around her two front teeth, hoping they'd grow closer together while she slept. It hadn't worked, though. Betsy's teeth were like pearls, small and white and even, without any spaces between them.

A gum wrapper glinted in the water ahead of her. Ruth bent down to fish it out, her slicker crackling. Later she'd peel away the paper backing and add the piece of tin foil to the ball they were making. When the ball got to be the size of a grapefruit, her father had said, they'd turn it in to the scrap drive. So far it was only as big as an apple.

The war certainly involved a lot of collecting—not only foil and flattened tin cans and bottle caps, but also newspapers and string and jars of fat. Ruth understood about saving metal and scrap paper. But what could the admirals and generals be planning to do with all those balls of string and people's leftover bacon grease?

Betsy had turned to see what Ruth was doing. "That's another thing that's backwards," she said grumpily as Ruth put the gum wrapper in her pocket. "People with braces aren't allowed to have gum, and you don't even like gum. It's just rotten luck." She sloshed on angrily. "Everything is rotten luck today. The Stewarts and the war and having to have meat loaf, and now *braces*."

Ruth didn't say anything. Privately she agreed, though she would have subtracted the meat loaf and added glasses, sixth grade, and having to go to Vickie Blair's party.

They were coming opposite the Selbys' house. Ruth sneaked a glance at it from under her hood, feeling somehow as if she shouldn't look, and saw that the black shades were still down.

The rain was letting up. In the vacant lot on the next corner, some little boys were playing with capguns, sneaking up on each other through the long, wet grass and yelling things like "Bang, bang, you're dead!" and "Got you, you dirty Hun!" Ruth's parents wouldn't allow them to play with guns, except for water pistols.

Betsy looked over her shoulder at the Selbys' house and said, "Do you think Alan killed any German soldiers before they killed him?"

Ruth shuddered. "I hope not."

"Well, that's what soldiers are supposed to do," Betsy pointed out as they turned the corner onto Spaulding Avenue. "That's why they have guns—to shoot at the other soldiers and kill them if they can.

I bet Alan didn't mind, though," she added. "He was mean. He liked to hurt people."

"You shouldn't say that," Ruth told her automatically, though she had an uneasy feeling that Betsy might be right.

"Not like Jack," Betsy said. "Jack liked people to be happy."

Ruth stopped short, staring at her sister's shiny yellow back.

Somehow she'd never thought about that part of it at all. She'd worried about Jack getting wounded or killed, but she hadn't ever imagined him pointing a gun at another person and taking aim and pulling the trigger and watching the person fall down with a bloody hole in him.

How could Jack be made to do such a thing— Jack, who was so easygoing and funny and popular, with friends always honking the horns of their jalopies for him and pretty girls calling him up on the telephone? Mrs. Buell used to shake her head over that, but Ruth didn't think she really minded. Did Jack's gentle, kindly parents ever picture how he'd have to act in the war—how he'd be using bullets and hand grenades and maybe even his bayonet to smash and hurt another human being? A boy his own age, maybe, who might be some other parents' only son?

Betsy had already crossed the strip of grass to the big green mailbox.

"Can I put the letter in?" she asked as Ruth came up. She looked surprised when Ruth nodded. They were fascinated by the way the box almost seemed to snatch at your fingers when you pulled back the heavy steel lip and fed an envelope into the slot. Sometimes they teased Carol by telling her a tiny postman lived down inside the box, ready to reach up and grab her and drag her down into the darkness, where there might be frogs and spiders and even snakes.

Ruth watched Betsy insert the letter and then jump back quickly in spite of herself, looking shamefaced.

She realized Betsy was too young to understand that what she'd just said about Jack Buell added up to the rottenest, most backwards thing of all. Ruth herself had thought she understood the worst thing about the war—that it was ordinary people dying, especially little children who'd had bombs dropped on their houses. But maybe she'd been wrong. Maybe killing was the worst thing

CHAPTER

~~~~~~~~~~~~~~~~~~~~~~~~~~~~~~~~~~~~~

ELEVEN

"Telephone for you, Ruth," her mother called. "Someone named Laura."

It was the next morning. Ruth had finally found her skate key and was sitting hunched over on the front steps, trying to adjust the clamp of her left skate so it would stay on without pinching her toes. She already had the right skate on.

"It's all right," her mother said from the doorway behind her, referring to the rule about not wearing roller skates in the house. "Just be careful on the rug."

Ruth set the left skate aside, slung the precious key around her neck, and stood up gingerly. Mrs. Owen looked at her watch and added with a frown, "I can't imagine what's happened to Miss Nitcomb. I told her I wanted to catch the 9:35."

She already had her hat and gloves on, ready to leave for the station. She was going into New York City to visit Randy Stewart in the hospital. First he'd been in a hospital here on Long Island, but then he'd been moved to one in New York. Miss Nitcomb was an elderly lady who lived on the next block with her even older sister and who sometimes took care of Ruth and her sisters when their parents weren't home.

"We'll be okay, Mom," Ruth assured her, clumping past her to the telephone. "We won't get into trouble or anything. And if we need someone before Miss Nitcomb comes, we can always go over to the Buells'."

Her mother hesitated, then looked at her watch again and sighed. "Well, all right. There's tuna fish salad in the icebox for your lunch. And tell Miss Nitcomb that Carol can have another Aspergum at eleven if she needs one."

Carol still had a sore throat, or at least she was pretending to—she loved Aspergum.

Between her mother's departure and the odd, unbalanced feeling of having one skate on and one off, Ruth barely had time to think that it must be Laura King on the phone before she picked up the receiver and said, "Hello."

"Hi, Ruth. This is Laura King. From Sunday school, remember?" She sounded nervous. Before Ruth could say sure, she remembered her, and also apologize for taking so long to answer the phone, Laura said, "What was that bumping sound?"

Ruth laughed. "That was me." She explained about her roller skate.

Laura said, "Oh, I love roller-skating. Only I'm not very good at it, because there weren't any sidewalks where we used to live. I used to skate in the driveway."

Ruth pulled up a chair and sat down, which made her feel less peculiar. When Laura didn't say anything more, she said, "Well, maybe we can skate together sometime"—not knowing if she really meant it—and added quickly, "Only not today, because we have someone taking care of us, and we can't have anyone over when she's here."

"Why not?" Laura asked. She didn't sound offended, just curious.

"Well, she's sort of old and shaky, and if too many things start happening at once, she has to go lie down on the couch and have us bring her a glass of ice water."

As she spoke, Ruth saw Miss Nitcomb hurrying up the front walk. Even though it was a warm morning and was supposed to get really hot later on, Miss Nitcomb was wearing her heavy navy-blue silk dress that looked as though it had been made for someone much larger.

"Excuse me a minute," Ruth said to Laura, and half-hopped, half-rolled to the door. "Hi, Miss Nitcomb," she said rapidly. "I'm on the phone, and Betsy and Carol are out in the backyard. Mom had to go catch her train."

"Oh, I'm so sorry to be late," Miss Nitcomb said

breathlessly. "What *must* your dear mother think of me? But my sister had one of her turns after breakfast—a pear I don't believe was quite ripe—" She broke off to stare distractedly at Ruth's feet. "Ruth, dear, ought you to be roller-skating inside the house? Somehow I don't think . . ."

"It's okay," Ruth told her, and waved her on into the kitchen as she returned to the telephone.

"Miss Nitcomb?" Laura said. Ruth could hear her trying not to laugh, and liked her for it. It *was* sort of a funny name, if you weren't used to it. "It sounds like you should be taking care of her, not the other way around." Now she did laugh.

Ruth grinned. "Well, in a way we are. She and her sister have hardly any money to live on," she explained, lowering her voice. "Also, she loves to play cards, but her sister is almost blind. She's taught Betsy and me some neat card games, like Casino and Russian Bank."

There was a silence. Then Laura cleared her throat and said, "Well, what I called about was to see if you could come over Saturday afternoon and maybe spend the night. My dad's going to cook hamburgers and hot dogs in the backyard, if it doesn't rain, and maybe take us all out for ice-cream cones after. Your parents could get you at church in the morning." She said all this in a rush, as if she'd practiced it.

Saturday was the day of Vickie Blair's party. Ruth would a thousand times rather go to Laura's, but she knew she couldn't, even though she still hadn't called Vickie, as she'd promised her mother she would. Nor could she tell Laura she'd been invited to a party that Laura wasn't invited to. That was practically her mother's number one politeness rule.

"I'd really like to," she told Laura sincerely, "but there's something else I have to do on Saturday."

"Oh. Well, if you can't . . . " Laura's voice trailed off. "I guess I'll see you in Sunday school, then," she said, and added, "I better get off the phone now. I'm calling from our neighbors' house, because we don't have a telephone yet. We were supposed to get one by now, but there's a shortage because of the war."

"The war is always messing things up," Ruth agreed quickly, feeling she shouldn't hang up just yet. She realized she'd hurt Laura's feelings, but she didn't know what to do about it. Without planning to, she found herself confessing, "I worry a lot about the boy that lives next door to us, Jack Buell. He's a soldier, and he might be in the Pacific now."

Laura said, "I know what you mean. One of my uncles is in the Marines, and my best friend at home's older brother is in the Navy. He's a Seabee." She giggled. "I know I shouldn't laugh, because what they do is really important and everything, but that's such a silly name, don't you think?"

Ruth smiled. "Like Kilroy," she said. No one knew who had started it or even what it meant, but all over Europe American soldiers had begun scrawling the message "Kilroy was here" on walls and doors and fences.

"Anyway," Laura went on, "my mom says we should concentrate on feeling proud of them instead of worrying so much. I mean, think how you'd feel if your neighbor was a draft-dodger. There was this one man in our town who pretended to have something wrong with his knee, when he was only double-jointed. And my grandfather had a hired man last year he was sure was hiding out from the draft, the way he'd moved around so much. Granddad was going to report him to the draft board, but before he could, the man quit. He just left, early in the morning, without even milking the cows. I think it's really rotten to be a draft-dodger, don't you?"

"Yes," Ruth said slowly, straightening the fringe of the hall rug with the rollers of her skate. She hated the thought that had sprung into her mind at Laura's words—that Russ, too, might be hiding from the draft. Well, you couldn't say he was hiding exactly, sitting up in his lifeguard's chair every day in full view of all the people on the beach. But what if the draft board had lost his address or something and didn't know where to find him? And what if Russ was glad about that?

Of course, it could be that Russ didn't believe in wars, even when they were to get rid of evil men like Hitler. Ruth knew there were people who refused to fight and would rather be put in jail instead. She'd thought that was just because they were scared. But now, with the ugly new picture in her mind of Jack Buell armed with a loaded rifle and a razor-sharp bayonet and a string of hand grenades on his belt (somehow the grenades were the worst), she understood that it might be because they hated the idea of hurting and killing so much.

"Ruth, are you still there?"

Laura's voice seemed to be coming from a great distance. Ruth discovered she'd let the receiver slide away from her ear. Hastily she slid it back and said, "Yes, but I better go now. See you on Sunday, okay?" Remembering her manners, she added, "And please thank your parents for inviting me over."

As soon as she hung up, she thought she should have asked Laura to go to the beach with them the next time they went. But she didn't know for sure when that would be. And she couldn't call Laura back, because she didn't know the neighbors' name or phone number. In fact, she didn't even know where Laura lived.

"Excuses," said a voice in her inner ear, as distinctly as a telephone voice with a good connection. She was almost glad to be distracted a moment later by Betsy stomping into the hall from the kitchen and declaring, "That's my skate key!"

"No, it isn't," Ruth told her, holding the key out on its cord and turning it over to show her. "There's no red mark."

"Maybe it wore off."

Ruth was happy for an excuse to get mad. "Betsy, I found this key in a shoe box in my closet, with my trading cards and my autograph book. How could it be *your* key?"

Betsy hung her head. "Well, I don't know where mine is." After a moment she mumbled, "Can I use yours when you're done with it?"

"If you give it right back. I don't want to get two blocks away and have my skate come off and not have my key."

Betsy scowled and turned away. "It's too hot to go roller-skating, anyway," she decided. "I'm going to go help Miss Nitcomb and Carol give Elinor a bath." Elinor was Carol's awful doll. "She said maybe we can go under the sprinkler later, as long as we don't get our hair wet."

The strap of Ruth's skate was hurting her ankle, and the little breeze that had been stirring the curtains at the side window seemed to have died away. Now she had to go skating, though, whether she felt like it or not. Besides, going under the sprinkler was for babies.

All the time she'd been sitting at the telephone table, she'd been trying not to see the invitation card tucked into the corner of the mirror above her. The pink frog continued to grin at her from its emerald-green lily pad. Quickly, before her heart could start pounding, telling herself that at least going to a swimming party was a grown-up kind of thing to do, Ruth plucked the card from the mirror and lifted the receiver.

CHAPTER

~~~~~~

TWELVE

The first thing Ruth did wrong was to go to the front door instead of heading directly around the back to the swimming pool.

As her father turned the Ford into the Blairs' semicircular driveway, a station wagon ahead of them was letting out a couple of boys. Whooping and yelling, they vanished onto a tree-shaded walk beside the house as the station wagon pulled away. But since she'd never been here before, Ruth thought she ought to ring the doorbell.

"I'll be back at five," her father told her as she got out of the car. "Now, Ruth," he said, looking at her. "You're going to have a good time."

She nodded wordlessly, clutching the rolled-up towel that contained her bathing suit and cap. On the phone Vickie had said to be sure to bring a bathing cap—it was one of their rules that girls couldn't go in the pool without one. She'd also said it wasn't a birthday party or anything, "just a get-together before school starts."

Three whole hours! Ruth tried not to think about that as she turned toward the shallow front steps, whose curve matched the curve of the driveway.

"You look very nice," her father added with an encouraging smile. He gave her the V-for-Victory sign before he drove away, tires crunching on the gravel.

The house was large and white, with two chimneys and a lot of green shutters. The inner door stood open, but Ruth couldn't see inside because the screen door made everything dark.

She took a deep breath, trying to stop the shuddering in her stomach. Before she lifted her hand to the doorbell, she checked to make sure her white blouse was still neatly tucked into her good powder blue shorts from Best & Company with the white stripe running down each side. Vickie had said not to dress up—everyone would just be coming in shorts.

Ruth was glad of that, at least. It was a hot, sultry afternoon, with thunder rumbling in the distance. She'd been watching the sky since early morning, hoping it would rain and they'd have to cancel the party. But the sky had remained smooth and pale, with nothing you could call a cloud.

After what seemed like a long time, a maid answered the doorbell. She was a large black woman wearing a starched blue uniform with a white collar and cuffs.

"You here for the party, honey?" she inquired, looking mildly surprised. "They're all around back, where the pool is."

"I guess I should have taken the path," Ruth stammered. "I'm Ruth Owen," she added, and stuck out her hand. "I hope I'm not late."

"Glad to know you, Ruth Owen," the woman said, shaking her hand gently. "I'm Sophie. Well, now, long as you're here, you might as well come on through the house. Lordy, ain't it hot today?" She fanned herself as she led Ruth through a dim, high-ceilinged hall. "Anyways, you ain't late, child. There's lots of folks still to come."

They went into a dining room, past a big, polished table bristling with chairs that Ruth kept her distance from in case they tripped her. A pair of tall doors opened onto a flagstone terrace. Beyond the terrace was an expanse of green lawn, and beyond that was the pool, a glittering rectangle of pale blue water with a long, low-roofed bathhouse at the far end.

No one was in swimming yet, though Ruth could make out several figures milling around among the chairs and tables in front of the bathhouse. She hesitated, dreading the walk across the lawn with everyone looking at her. If only she'd taken the path, she would have been shielded by trees and bushes until the very last part.

As if Sophie guessed what she was feeling, she gave Ruth's shoulder a little squeeze and observed,

"Got some nice refreshments for later, when you all get tired of swimming. You like those little egg-salad sandwiches with the crusts cut off?"

Ruth nodded. She adored egg sandwiches, at least she did in her other life—her real life, where she was always hungry. Today she hadn't been able to eat any lunch, only a saltine and a sip of milk her mother made her have before she left.

"Well, ain't nobody makes a better egg sandwich than me," Sophie assured her. After a pause, she asked kindly, "You see anyone there you know, honey?"

Ruth shook her head. "I'm nearsighted," she explained miserably. At the moment, she would have been glad to recognize even Mary Jo Douglas, with her loud laugh and stringy hair. She squared her shoulders, said, "Well, I guess I'll see you later, Sophie," tucked her rolled-up towel under her arm, and forced herself to cross the terrace and go down the steps.

She was halfway across the lawn when Mrs. Blair saw her and came hurrying the length of the pool to greet her. She was a thin, blond woman wearing a flowered beach coat and espadrilles and dark glasses, like a movie star.

Ruth's heart sank. The only thing worse than arriving at a party alone was having the mother lead you around and introduce you to everyone, so they all had to stop talking.

Sure enough, Mrs. Blair took Ruth's hand and said brightly, "You must be Ruth. I've seen you from a distance with your mother"—making it plain why Ruth had been invited. "Where's that daughter of mine? Vickie, come say hello to Ruth." She drew Ruth toward the end of the pool and announced, "This is Ruth Owen, everyone. She's going to be in your grade this year. Isn't that right, dear?"

There were six guests at the party so far, already changed into their bathing suits—four girls and the two boys Ruth had seen arriving earlier. They stared at Ruth as Mrs. Blair rattled off their names. Two of the girls said "hi" without enthusiasm.

Vickie was back in a kind of kitchenette that separated the two sides of the bathhouse, opening bottles of soda and bags of pretzels and potato chips. She gave Ruth a friendly smile over her shoulder and said, "Hi, Ruth, glad you could come." Vickie was blond like her mother, with her hair cut in a perfect pageboy. She wore a two-piece white bathing suit that made her skin look the golden color of perfectly done toast.

She added to one of the boys, "Hey, Brian, you better watch out if you still want to be at the head of the class. Ruth skipped a grade, so she must be really smart."

Brian was skinny and redheaded and not much taller than Ruth, which should have made her feel better, but his expression was anything but welcoming. He studied her for a moment with flat, greenish eyes, then shrugged and helped himself to a handful of potato chips.

"Oh, who wants to think about *school*,"

exclaimed one of the girls, tossing a head of short, glossy brown curls. "It's so hot! Can we go in the pool now, Mrs. Blair?"

"Yes, I suppose so," Mrs. Blair said distractedly, as a group of new arrivals appeared along the flagstone path. "My husband promised to be here to help lifeguard, but since it looks as though he's still out on the golf course . . ."

"Oh, Mom, we don't need a lifeguard!" Vickie protested. "Everyone knows how to swim."

"Well, as long as there's no roughhousing, and only one person on the diving board at a time . . ." Mrs. Blair turned to Ruth, still standing awkwardly beside one of the padded lounge chairs with her towel under her arm. "Why don't you run along and change, dear, before things get too crowded. Take the door on the right—that's the girls' side. Your mother tells me you're a fine little swimmer," she added with an encouraging smile.

Ruth cringed, but attention was diverted from her by the other boy, Richard, who ran the length of the diving board, bounced high in the air, and hit the water in a cannonball that produced an enormous splash.

She hurried into the dressing room, hoping it would have separate cubicles. But there was just a bench with a mirror over it and some hooks for people's clothes. Wanting to get changed before anyone else came in, Ruth shucked off her blouse and shorts and tugged on her bathing suit, almost stumbling in her haste.

She avoided her reflection in the mirror, not wanting to see how babyish the suit looked, besides being all stretched out and faded. The bold yellow zigzag was only a faint pattern now against the washed-out blue. Then she thought of all the big waves she'd dived through in this same bathing suit, and felt comforted.

When she came out, Vickie was talking and laughing with some girls who'd just arrived. Ruth knew one of them, Ellen Collier, from air-raid drills at school, but she couldn't think of anything to say to her. She and Ellen had both been homeroom captains last year, in charge of counting kids in and out of the basement and making sure everyone had a kit of quiet things to do. That was in case the air raid turned out to be a real one and they had to stay down in the gloomy cement corridors for more than the usual ten minutes.

The girls went inside to change, and Vickie turned and handed Ruth a Coke. The heavy green bottle was so slick with condensation that Ruth almost let it slip through her fingers. She set it down quickly on a table and told Vickie, "No, thank you."

"We have ginger ale, too, if you'd rather," Vickie said, looking at her curiously.

It was true that Ruth's parents didn't like them to drink Coca-Cola, saying it was bad for their teeth, but that wasn't why Ruth had refused. She said, "Shouldn't we wait to eat until after we've been in swimming?"

Vickie frowned. "Why?"

Ruth realized she'd made another mistake. She looked down at the bathing cap in her hand—a new one, chalky white, made of some thin, stretchy synthetic because of the rubber shortage—and said lamely, "Well, it's just a rule in our family."

The curly-haired girl was sitting on the edge of the pool, munching a pretzel. She looked around and said with a giggle, "What's the matter, are they afraid you'll get a nasty old cramp and drown?"

Richard, the boy who'd jumped off the diving board, was climbing up the ladder at the corner of the pool. Now he flopped back into the water, pretended to sink, and came up crying, "Help, help, Mommy, I've got a tummyache" in a high, squeaky voice. He let himself sink again, while everyone laughed.

The curly-haired girl said teasingly, "Hey, Ruth, I dare you to eat a pretzel."

"Two pretzels," someone said.

"No, no, two might sink her." This was Brian, his green eyes gleaming with malice.

"Come on, you guys," Vickie said reproachfully.

Ruth made herself smile, though her cheeks were burning. "Well, I guess I'll get wet," she said, and walked away to the shallow end of the pool. Behind her she could hear Vickie saying something to the others in a low voice. She went down the shallow steps into the water, sure that all eyes were on her. But when she looked up from fastening the strap of her bathing cap, no one was even facing her way. The new arrivals had come out of the bathhouse and were helping themselves to refreshments, while Mrs. Blair was greeting yet another group of guests coming along the flagstone path.

The water was much warmer than Ruth had expected, almost like bathwater from all the hot weather they'd been having. She swam the length of the pool and back again, keeping to the side away from the steps at one end and the ladder at the other. Then, because she couldn't think of anything else to do, she started another lap. This time she almost collided with two girls who were floating on their backs, talking. Changing direction, she struck out on a diagonal toward the corner where the ladder was, and just missed being jumped on by Richard, doing another cannonball off the diving board.

"Hi, Ruth," a voice said in her ear as she clung to the edge of the pool, trying to plot a path back to the shallow end. It was Ellen Collier, almost unrecognizable without her glasses and with her long, dark hair tucked out of sight beneath her cap.

"I just heard you're going to be in our grade this year. That's neat! Do you know what teacher you have?"

"Miss Amory," Ruth told her shyly.

"So do I," Ellen said, looking pleased. Ellen had the right kind of face for glasses, Ruth thought enviously—broad cheekbones and a wide mouth. In fact, she almost looked better with her glasses on than without them. "Let's go down to the other end, okay? It's too crowded here. Unless you want to go on the diving board."

Ruth shook her head. "I don't really know how to dive," she said, "except through waves."

She didn't think Ellen heard that last part, though, because she'd turned her face away to avoid being splashed by a beefy, straw-haired boy who was diving into the pool over their heads. It was getting very noisy. Mr. Blair had arrived and was yelling at two boys to quit ducking each other, standing back from the tiled edge of the pool to keep his plaid golfing pants from getting wet.

"Vickie must have invited the whole sixth grade," Ellen said as they edged their way to the shallow end. "We better not have a thunderstorm like the radio said—we'd never all fit under that little roof." She looked at the bathhouse, adding uneasily, "I guess we shouldn't be near a pool anyway, if there's lightning. I hate thunderstorms, don't you?"

Ruth nodded, though actually she thought they were kind of fun. Ellen sat down on the middle step, hugging her knees, and Ruth sat beside her, though she was so much smaller the water almost came up to her chin.

She, too, felt uneasy, but she wasn't sure just why. Ellen was telling her about some of the other kids— who was okay when you got to know them (Janice, the curly-haired girl) and who was mean (Brian) or stupid (Don, the big boy with the spiky blond hair).

Ruth tried to listen, but somehow she couldn't concentrate. She looked at the pool, which seemed to have shrunk in the half hour since she'd first seen it, clear and shining at the end of the lawn. It was so full of kids now that there wasn't any room for swimming, and the churned-up water had a dull, soapy look.

She stood up abruptly. "I think I'll get out for a while," she told Ellen.

Ellen looked surprised. "Why? At least it's cooler in the water than out of it."

"I know, but—" Ruth shook her head and backed up the steps.

Suddenly all she could think of was how crowded the pool had become, more like a public pool than a private one. The Stewart boys hadn't gotten polio from going in a pool, she was pretty sure. Still, it was David who'd gotten sick first, and then passed the germ to his younger brothers. Now David was all right, and Jonathan would be, too, except for a weak leg that would probably get stronger in time. But Randy wouldn't ever run again, or ride his tricycle around in circles, or do silly somersaults in the snow. What if that should happen to Carol, all because of Ruth and her everlasting rotten luck?

"Oh, there you are, Ruth!"

As Ruth stood dripping on the tiles, tugging at the strap of her bathing cap—which suddenly felt much too tight, almost making her gasp for breath— Mrs. Blair appeared at her elbow, smiling her bright, hostessy smile.

"I thought in a few minutes we might clear the pool and have some relay races, boys against girls. You're such a good little swimmer, perhaps you'd like to be captain of the girls' team?"

But all Ruth wanted now was to get away from the pool with its close-packed, squirming bodies, its warm, cloudy water sloshing back and forth like water in a mop bucket.

The snap on her bathing cap was new and stiff. She yanked the strap free at last, with an effort that almost made her stagger. And that was when the third wrong thing happened. As she stripped off the cap and turned blindly away onto the grass, Ruth crashed headlong into Sophie, coming across the lawn with a tray of sandwiches and two tall glass pitchers of lemonade.

CHAPTER

~~~~~~~~~~~~~~~~~~~~~~~~~~~~~~

THIRTEEN

"And that's how I cut my foot," she told Russ forlornly the next day. "It was just a little piece of glass that didn't go in very far, but it bled a whole lot." She sighed. "At least no one else cut themselves."

Though it might have been easier if someone else had, she couldn't help thinking, remembering the silence that had followed the crash. All the bodies in the pool had stopped moving, except for heads turning to stare. Then some of the kids started laughing. Well, they probably *had* looked pretty funny—Ruth hopping up and down and clutching at Sophie in her spattered uniform, Mrs. Blair on her knees, hands fluttering as she tried to decide which to do first, pick up the broken glass or retrieve the sandwiches from the grass.

"Well, hey, it was just an accident, right?" Russ said. "I mean, it's the kind of thing that could happen to anyone."

Ruth hadn't told him the real reason she'd been in such a hurry to leave the pool. She only said she'd been feeling sick. She was ashamed of her panic now, and thought maybe she really had been kind of sick, from the heat and not eating any lunch and not wanting to be at Vickie's party in the first place.

She bent over and gave a tug to the cotton sock her parents were making her wear over the Band-Aid on her instep. They'd allowed her to go in swimming, saying salt water would be good for the cut, but they didn't want her to get sand in it.

Seeing Ruth hobbling around, Russ had called to her and invited her to sit up in the chair with him for a while. He wasn't supposed to have company, he'd said with a grin, but Ruth wouldn't take up much room, and maybe she could help keep the sand flies off him. It was another hot, windless day—so hot back on Kempton Street that Ruth's parents had decided to skip church that morning and go straight to the beach. The predicted thunderstorm had never happened, and the sky was once again a pale, cloudless blue.

In spite of her confused feelings about Russ maybe being a draft-dodger, Ruth was glad to see him again. Telling him about the party hadn't made her feel better, though. Instead, it made it seem to be happening all over again, even more painfully—

as sharp in her memory as the feeling of the glass sliver piercing her foot.

"I wish I never had to see any of those kids again," she muttered.

"Well, sure, I can see how you might feel that way." Russ shifted on the cushion, and Ruth looked quickly to see if she was crowding him. But there was plenty of room, as long as she held the megaphone and the binoculars on her lap.

"But hey, Ruth, they've probably forgotten all about it by now. It seems like a big, embarrassing thing to you, but to them it's just one of a whole bunch of things that happened at the party. And it's not like you're naturally clumsy. Once they get to know you better—" He shrugged.

Ruth shook her head. "You don't know what they're like, some of them. There's this one boy named Brian . . . "

She swallowed hard and sat staring out at the gleaming steel blue skin of the ocean, rippling like the back of a whale. There were some big waves far out, but otherwise the water was calm, with just a frill of white along the shore.

"The only person I liked at the whole party was Sophie," she said after a while. "And Ellen, I guess."

Another tall girl, she thought morosely, though not quite as tall as Laura King. That reminded her she was missing Sunday school today and wouldn't be seeing Laura as she'd told her she would. Oh, well, Laura would be better off not having Ruth for a friend anyway, now that she'd made a fool of herself in front of practically the whole sixth grade.

"Sophie?" Russ said.

"The maid," Ruth explained. She added, "I found out she has two children down South that she hardly ever gets to see. When they were little, she came up North to work, so she could send them money and keep them in school till they grew up. The boy might even go to college, if the war gets over in time."

It was Sophie who had helped Ruth across the lawn to the house, where she'd removed the sliver of glass with a pair of tweezers, washed out the cut, and wrapped a clean rag around Ruth's foot. While Ruth waited for her father to come get her, she'd sat at the kitchen table with her leg propped on a chair, watching Sophie make more egg sandwiches and squeeze lemons for a new batch of lemonade.

She'd felt bad about that, but Sophie said only one pitcher had broken and that she still had more lemons than she knew what to do with—eggs, too. And although Ruth was sure she'd lost her appetite forever, she'd ended up eating half a dozen of the little sandwiches, which were just as delicious as Sophie had said they'd be. She even had a slice of chocolate layer cake that wasn't supposed to be for the party.

"It's not fair," Ruth said now, sliding down on her spine and glowering out at the ocean. "Why do things have to be so hard for colored people? And now, after all Sophie's work and being so lonely and everything, what if her son has to go in the Army and maybe get killed? It's just rotten luck, that's all."

She hadn't meant to mention the Army to Russ, but he didn't seem disturbed. He said, "Well, maybe none of that will happen," and punched her lightly on the upper arm. "Come on, Ruth, cheer up. You're here at the beach where you love to be, remember? And it's still summer. Another couple of weeks before school starts. A lot can happen in two weeks—good things, I mean."

Ruth nodded, although she couldn't think of any. The only two things she knew were going to happen were that she had an appointment with the eye doctor next Wednesday and that Joan was going to come home and tell her how much fun she'd had in New Hampshire.

She raised Russ's binoculars to her eyes and fiddled with the lenses until the focus cleared. She found herself looking at two small pairs of legs sticking out of the water some distance from shore. A sandbar, she realized after a moment, and a couple of kids standing on their hands. She smiled in spite of herself at how silly they looked.

Then the heads came up, and Ruth saw that one pair of legs belonged to her sister Betsy and the other to Betsy's friend Cindy. She was surprised to see Betsy out so far. Then she realized that the binoculars made the big waves beyond Betsy look much closer than they really were, looming like mountain peaks with snow spilling down their steep slopes.

The binoculars were heavy. After another moment Ruth lowered them again.

"Well, I hope *you* never have to go in the Army," she told Russ, having made up her mind about that much at least. When he didn't say anything, only frowned a little, she explained, "I don't mean just because of being in danger, but because—well, you wouldn't want to hurt someone else, would you, someone you didn't even know? I think it's much better to save people, like you do."

"I guess it would depend on the circumstances," Russ said, taking the binoculars from her. "If someone was trying to kill one of my buddies, or if it was a choice between killing and getting killed—"

He broke off suddenly and thrust the binoculars back into Ruth's lap. "Hold the fort, okay? Looks like I may have a little job to do."

Before Ruth could respond, he'd swung himself down onto the sand and was running toward the water with an odd, lurching gait that Ruth noticed with one part of her mind. The other was busy refocusing the binoculars so that she could see what Russ had been looking at.

There were a number of swimmers in the calm water beyond the sandbar, most of them just floating in the swells or practicing their strokes. One of them, though, seemed to be doing a lot of splashing, twisting and turning and thrashing around as if something had her by the legs.

Ruth froze as the small head came into focus. It was Betsy who was in trouble! Clearly now,

108

seeming so close that Ruth felt she should be able to reach out and touch her, she could see Betsy's white, scared face. Her eyes were squinched shut, and her squared-down mouth kept gasping for breath as she swallowed water and tried to spit it out again.

Quickly, Ruth scanned toward shore and saw Betsy's dumb friend Cindy wading through the shallows, patting the small waves with her hands, not even looking over her shoulder. Where was Dad?

CHAPTER

~~~~~~~~~~~~~~~~~~~~~~~~~~~~~~~~

FOURTEEN

Clutching the binoculars, Ruth jumped down from the chair, barely noticing the jolt to her injured foot as she hit the sand. Russ was swimming powerfully on a long diagonal toward Betsy, swimming faster than anyone Ruth had ever seen except for Johnny Weissmuller in the newsreels— and Russ didn't even have his face in the water. Instead, he was holding his head up in order to keep Betsy in sight.

Awkwardly, trying to steady the binoculars against her eyes as she ran, Ruth angled down the slope of the beach into the water and almost collided with her mother, who was standing in the frill of surf gripping Carol by the hand. Through the binoculars, Ruth saw that her father was out on the sandbar now, standing up tall while he yelled something to Betsy through his cupped hands. "Float!" he was calling. "Float, Betsy! Wait for the swell and just let the water carry you."

"It's okay," Ruth said breathlessly over the thudding of her heart. "Russ will get her."

Her mother nodded tensely. Ruth offered the binoculars to her, but she waved them away. "I can see. He's almost there . . . ah, he's got her." Her shoulders sagged, and she let out a long, shuddery breath.

"Ow, Mommy, you're hurting my hand!" Carol complained.

"Sorry," her mother said, releasing it. "Your father was swimming without his glasses," she explained to Ruth. "He probably saw Cindy come in and thought Betsy was with her. But Betsy was so far out—and those enormous waves . . ."

"They're miles away, though," Ruth said.

"I know, but if Betsy got scared . . ." Mrs. Owen shook her head.

So her mother knew about Betsy's being scared of the ocean, Ruth realized in surprise. She raised the binoculars again, then realized she didn't need them. Russ and Betsy had almost reached the sandbar. He wasn't towing her, the way Ruth had sometimes seen lifeguards do, holding the person's chin or wrapping an arm around their chest. Instead, he was swimming on his back with Betsy's hands resting on his shoulders, and they seemed to be talking.

"What's happening?" Cindy demanded, wading over to them and wringing the water from the ruffled skirt of her bathing suit. "Why are you all standing here?"

Ruth exchanged a glance with her mother. She thought how embarrassed Betsy was going to be, and wondered if her mother was thinking the same thing. Before they could say anything, though, Cindy turned and looked out at the sandbar, where Russ was just handing Betsy to her father. "Ooh," she said, "did Betsy have to get *rescued*?"

"She just got a little tired," Mrs. Owen said firmly.

"Ooh," Cindy exclaimed again. "The lucky! I wish that would happen to me sometime. Is the lifeguard gonna have to carry her out of the water and do that thing where they make you lie down on the sand and start pushing on your ribs?"

Not for the first time, Ruth decided Cindy was a real dope. "Oh, Cindy, don't be dumb," she said. "Betsy's fine. Look."

Russ and her father were swimming slowly in from the sandbar now, with Betsy doing the elementary backstroke between them. Mrs. Owen started to wade toward them, then seemed to think better of it. Instead, she said briskly, "All right, Carol, if you're going to have a swim, you'd better do it now. It's almost time for lunch. And Cindy, you look cold. Go on up and dry off. We'll be along in a minute."

After Cindy had turned away, Ruth splashed through a couple of small waves and swam out to join the others. The water felt cold after all the time she'd spent sitting in the sun, and the sock dragged at her foot.

"I think you can touch bottom now, Betsy," her father was saying, standing up himself in waist-high water. He turned to Russ and shook his hand. "Good thing you were keeping an eye out," he said with a grimace. "Ought to know better than to swim without my glasses, but they're a darned nuisance. No matter how I try to tie them on, they're always falling off."

"Oh, I don't think Betsy was in any real danger," Russ said in his easy way. "There might have been a bit of rip current, though. Just as well to play it safe."

Betsy was trying to smile, but her teeth were chattering.

"I got sort of turned around," she said, looking at Ruth. "I meant to be coming back in, but then the water was so deep, and there were all those big waves up in the sky . . ."

Ruth thought how she herself had panicked at Vickie's party.

"Yes," she agreed. "I sure wouldn't want to try and dive through one of *those.*"

Russ gave her a quick little nod of approval, as if he knew what she'd been thinking. "Hey, Ruth, I thought I told you to hold the fort," he teased, nodding in the direction of the lifeguard's chair.

She clapped a hand to her mouth. "Oh, your binoculars! I left them on the beach—at least I hope

I did." As she plunged back through the water, she heard her father say to Betsy, "Hey, how about a piggyback ride?" and saw him boost her onto his shoulders. Betsy squealed, sounding more like her usual self.

The binoculars were lying in the wet sand at the water's edge where Ruth had dropped them. Luckily they were too heavy to have been carried off by a wave. She rinsed them off and turned to give them to Russ, who had waded along behind her. He seemed to stumble as he reached for them, steadying himself with a hand on Ruth's shoulder.

"Hey, you didn't cut yourself on something, did you?" she asked in concern. "That's all we need— both of us with a cut foot."

Russ smiled and shook his head, slinging the binoculars around his neck. Now it was Ruth's turn to steady herself against him while she took off her sock, emptied the sand out of it, and pulled it on again. When they came out of the water, though, Russ was still limping.

"Hey—" Ruth said again, and stopped.

Now she could see that there was something wrong with Russ's left leg. It was a little thinner than the other, something she'd never noticed when he was sitting up in the chair. There was something funny about his hip on that side, too—it turned out more than it should.

Ruth stood stunned, watching Russ move up the slope of the beach. His left foot dragged behind him, scuffing against the sand and causing him to put his weight stiffly on his other leg—his good leg.

She hurried to catch up with him, clutching his hand and staring up wide-eyed into his face.

"Yeah, I realized you didn't know," he said gruffly. "You never saw me do anything but sit, right? I should have told you, I guess, but . . ." He shrugged. "It's not such an easy thing to work into a conversation." He gave her hand a little shake and said, "Hey, pal, don't look at me that way! One leg's a bit shorter than the other, that's all. I manage okay—not too gracefully, I guess, but it looks worse than it is."

Still speechless, Ruth trailed after him as he covered the remaining distance to the chair, noticing how people on the beach stared for a moment and then looked quickly away. She wished furiously that the fat man, the one with the murderous umbrella, was here to see him.

With a swift, practiced movement, Russ hoisted himself up into the chair. No wonder his arms were so strong, Ruth thought.

Finding her voice at last, she said, "Is it . . . was it from polio?"

He nodded, settling himself on the seat and looking around for his sailor's hat. "When I was twelve. In fact, the doctors didn't think I was ever going to walk again, so I figure I'm way ahead of the game." He put the cap on at a jaunty angle and grinned down at her. "Also, it keeps me on the home front, as you noticed."

With his white cap tilted against the blue sky, Russ looked exactly like the smiling sailor in one of the posters urging people to buy war bonds.

Ruth said hesitantly, "Do you mind about that?"

He shrugged. "Well, I guess I'd like to be part of it." Like her father, Ruth thought. "But you're right that I'd just as soon not get shot at, let alone have to shoot someone else."

Ruth sank down on the sand in front of the chair, feeling hot with shame that she'd ever supposed Russ could be a draft-dodger. "The way you were swimming just now," she said after a moment. "I never saw anyone swim that fast."

"Water therapy," Russ explained, his eyes scanning the ocean in their steady, methodical way. "You know how the President had a pool put in at the White House?" Ruth nodded. "Well, swimming's one of the best things you can do if you've had polio. The minute I heard that, there was no keeping me out of the big pool at the hospital where I was." He laughed. "I made the nurses roll me down and tip me in, and I never came out until they made me. Talk about blue lips and goose bumps!"

Ruth still couldn't even smile. "Didn't it hurt?" she asked.

"Oh, hurt . . ." Russ shrugged, as if that didn't matter. "Well, sure. But if you want something badly enough, you go after it. My family helped a lot, too, my big brother especially. He'd take me to the pool—this was after I was back·home again—

and when he'd see I was getting tired, he'd bet me I couldn't do one more lap." Russ shook his head. "He'd yell stuff about how I was a coward and a sissy, and if I didn't watch out, I'd wind up being a no-good, useless cripple for the rest of my life."

"That's terrible!" Ruth said, staring up at him.

"Yeah, I used to think so too, and I'd get mad as heck at him. But inside . . ." Russ paused. "Well, I guess I knew he just wanted me to be the best I could be. I mean, suppose he'd said, 'Great, Russ, you're doing fine, why don't you take a rest now'? I might never have gotten this far." He grinned. "Tony's in the Air Corps now, a bombardier. I bet his crew never stops hearing it from him."

Ruth was silent, trying to decide if Tony was a person she would have liked. She hoped he hadn't asked to be made a bombardier.

Russ gave her a thoughtful glance and said, "It's sort of like what your parents are doing to you, maybe."

She frowned and looked away. "It's not the same," she said, picking at a scab on her knee. She'd gotten it roller-skating last week, when she'd taken a corner too fast and gone down in a heap. Miss Nitcomb had insisted on painting the scrape with mercurochrome, though Ruth would have preferred iodine—it stung more, but it also worked better.

Russ seemed to be waiting for her to go on. She said haltingly, "They don't know how I feel inside. About being shy and small for my age, I mean, and always having to act like the oldest and be grown-up with my sisters, even when I don't feel like it. Well, maybe my dad understands, but my mom doesn't. She's too different from me."

"I bet she does. Being different doesn't necessarily mean you can't understand." When Ruth didn't say anything, Russ said, "About that party yesterday."

She looked up at him, feeling her skin go clammy again at the thought of all the kids staring at her and laughing—and even worse, at the prospect of having to face them again on the first day of school. She'd been been thinking she might be able to hide in the girls' room until the bell rang, and then creep into a chair at the back of the room. At least with her new glasses, she thought bitterly, she'd be able to see the blackboard from there.

Russ said, "Sounds to me like you got boiled."

Ruth smiled reluctantly, because that was exactly what it had felt like—like getting up your nerve and plunging into a big, scary wave, thinking you were going to be okay, and then getting boiled after all.

"So okay," Russ prompted. "What do you do next? Let's say you stand up, you're all dizzy and sore from being knocked around—and right away there's another big wave hanging over you."

Ruth knew what he wanted her to say, but somehow it was hard to get the words out.

"Dive through it, I guess," she said at last.

"You *guess*? Hey, you've got no other choice." Russ grinned at her, shifting in the chair in the way she knew now probably meant that his hip was

118

hurting. "Maybe you'll get boiled again, but you'll get boiled even worse if you don't try."

Ruth thought about this—about all the bad-luck waves that could rise out of nowhere to smash people down, and how Russ had gotten boiled in one of the biggest waves of all.

She wanted to tell him she thought he was as brave as any soldier charging up a hill against enemy fire, any sailor watching a torpedo speed toward his ship. But before she could find the words, he glanced along the beach and said, "Hey, I see your folks waving at you. Time for lunch, maybe?"

Ruth nodded and pushed herself to her feet. "Spam sandwiches," she grumbled, then shrugged a bit sheepishly. "Actually, I kind of like Spam," she confessed, "even if everyone else hates it."

"With plenty of mustard," Russ agreed. "So do I. But then, we're probably both a little peculiar, you and me." This time his smile was as wide as the brim of his sailor's hat, and Ruth noticed for the first time that there was a small gap between his two front teeth. "Better put a new Band-Aid on that cut," he advised. "I don't think that sorry-looking sock can be doing much good any more."

"Aye, aye, sir," Ruth said, smiling back.

She started to turn away, then thought of something. Even though it hurt to put her full weight on her cut foot, she drew herself stiffly to attention and gave Russ a salute—a real salute with a snap to it, like she'd seen Jack Buell practicing before he went away.

CHAPTER

～～～～～～～～～～

FIFTEEN

As she limped back along the beach, zigzagging around the families on their blankets and the little kids burying each other in the sand, Ruth wondered if the Stewarts knew about swimming, for Randy. If they didn't, she'd get her parents to tell them.

She also found herself wondering if Laura King's family had gotten their telephone by now. If they had, she could probably get the number from Information. It was always fun to tell the operator, "Information, please," and then listen while she rustled through the pages of some special phone book and finally recited the number in a voice that sounded like someone talking through a hole in a tin can.

Yes, Ruth thought with a sudden surge of energy,

maybe she'd try calling Laura when she got home. And if the Kings still didn't have a telephone, she could get their address from Mrs. Morgan or Mrs. Graham and ask her mother to drive her there, if it was too far to walk or ride her bike.

In fact, maybe Laura could come to the beach with them some day next week. That would give them both a chance to get used to the difference in their sizes and see if they really liked each other. Ruth might even tell Laura about Vickie's party. She had a feeling it would make Laura laugh, at least if she told it the right way. Laura would have to watch out for getting sunburned, though, with her light hair and all those freckles. Ruth made a mental note to ask Russ for the name of the white stuff he put on his nose.

"There you are!"

Her mother was pouring milk into the battered metal thermos cups, saving the biggest one for Ruth. She looked up with a smile and said, "I was afraid you'd lost your appetite."

Maybe because of what Russ had said, Ruth saw the concern behind the smile. She smiled back, shaking her head, and reached for a Spam sandwich.

"Careful!" her father said as she flopped down on the old steamer rug between Betsy and Carol. Ruth looked and saw she'd almost sat on his glasses. She handed them to him and watched him hook them carefully over his ears. Immediately they became part of his face again.

As she ate her sandwich, she remembered the page from a ladies' magazine that Joan had enclosed in her last letter. It showed different shapes of faces and a row of differently shaped eyeglass frames. The directions said to trace the frames and then try them on the face whose shape matched your own, to see the kind of glasses that would look best on you. Or you could draw the glasses on a snapshot of yourself, if you had a special kind of grease pencil.

Ruth had barely glanced at the page, telling herself Joan was just trying to rub it in about her having to wear glasses. Now she admitted that Joan was only trying to help. When she got home today—maybe even before she called Laura—she'd take a piece of tracing paper and try out each frame on the face that was the longest and narrowest. The magazine said you could also draw your hair around the face. That would be easy enough in Ruth's case, since all she'd need were a few straight lines.

This reminded her of Ellen Collier, who really did look good in glasses. She thought how Ellen hadn't laughed when Ruth broke the pitcher; instead, she'd scrambled out of the pool to see if she could help, only to be waved away distractedly by Mrs. Blair.

If only Ellen weren't so tall.

Ruth grinned suddenly at the picture that had just formed in her mind. If she made friends with both Laura and Ellen, she'd look even shrimpier than she already did. On the other hand, the three of them together might look funny ha-ha instead of funny peculiar—almost as if Ruth were a kind of mascot. Everyone liked mascots, even in the Army. At least they did in the comic strips, where the short guy was always the spunky one who made the others laugh and who had all the good ideas.

"Feeling better?" Her father patted her on the knee, sprinkling some grains of sand in her cup of milk.

Ruth didn't mind. What was a picnic at the beach without sand? She nodded slowly, knowing he didn't mean just her cut foot, and looked out to sea.

The big waves loomed against the horizon, still keeping their distance from shore. Meanwhile the sun burned hot on the top of Ruth's head and dazzled like a million silver coins on the gently heaving surface of the water. The briny smell of the ocean prickled her nostrils, and her ears were full of the slur and swish of small waves breaking along the miles of sand.

She turned to her mother. "Can I have the other half of Betsy's sandwich if she doesn't want it?" Betsy hated Spam.

Carol said, "I might want it."

Ruth glared at her. Their father said in a resigned voice, "Pick a number between one and twenty."

"No," Carol said suddenly. "Ruth can have it."

"Thanks," Ruth said, and gave her little sister her biggest smile, the one she knew showed the space between her front teeth. She took another bite of

Spam—saltier even than the sea—washed it down with a swallow of sandy milk, and heaved a sigh of contentment.

"I didn't even think I was hungry," she told her family. "But all of a sudden I'm starved!"

About the Author

Mary Towne is the author of nine novels for young readers. Her most recent middle-grade books are *Wanda the Worrywart, Steve the Sure,* and *Their House*, which was praised by Kirkus Reviews as "an unusual novel that addresses the real problems of the elderly while involving readers with several memorable, vividly drawn characters."

Ms. Towne was born in Brooklyn, New York, and lived on Long Island (the setting of *Dive Through the Wave*) until she was twelve. She and her husband now make their home in the mountains of western North Carolina—"the farthest I've ever lived from the ocean, but the mountains help make up for that."